AUGHTER

SYBIL COOK

ANNIE

"You need to put more wax on that stitch, girl. A merchant like Mr. Walter expects his boots to last through three winters."

Annie looked up from her work and pushed a loose strand of hair back from her face. "Yes, Pa. I know." She dipped her fingers into the small tin of beeswax and ran it along the thick thread. The boots on her lap belonged to one of their last good customers.

"Mr. Walter pays top price. We can't afford to lose his business," her father called from across the shop.

"I know, Pa." Annie bent closer to her work, focusing on the neat line of stitches she was placing along the sole. Her fingers moved with the skill that came from years of practice, though her mind wandered to their dwindling stack of bills hidden in the old tea tin.

The bell above the door jingled, and Annie looked up to see her friend Molly step inside. Molly's cheeks were pink from the cold, and she carried a small cloth bundle.

"Morning, Mr. Sutherland. Morning, Annie," Molly said with a smile.

"Molly Peters." Annie's father nodded from his workbench. "What brings you to our shop today?"

"I brought some meat pies from our kitchen," Molly said, placing the bundle on the counter. "Ma made extra this morning and thought you might like some."

Annie set aside her work and stood up. "Thank you, Molly. That's very kind."

"It's nothing," Molly said, unwrapping the cloth to reveal two still-warm pies. "How's business?"

Annie felt her smile tighten. "It's..."

"It's as good as can be expected with those factory boots taking all our customers," her father cut in, pointing toward the window.

Annie walked to Molly's side, and they both

looked out across the street. A cart had pulled up to the general store, and men were unloading crates. Mr. Thompson, the store owner, stood watching with his hands on his hips and a big smile on his face.

"What's that?" Molly asked.

"New shipment of factory boots," Annie said, keeping her voice low. "They sell them for half what we charge."

"But they can't be as good as yours," Molly protested.

Annie shrugged. "They're good enough for most people, it seems."

They watched as a group of men stopped to look at the crates. One pointed to the shop sign showing the price.

"Five shillings for boots?" one man said loud enough for them to hear through the glass. "That's less than half what Sutherland charges!"

Annie turned away from the window. "Would you like some tea, Molly?"

"I can't stay long. I have to get back to the sewing shop." Molly hesitated. "Mrs. Davis said she might need help with some extra work this week. I could ask if she needs another pair of hands."

"I'm a cobbler, not a seamstress," Annie said.

"You have good hands for stitching," Molly said. "And Mrs. Davis pays fair."

"We're not that desperate yet," Annie's father called, then broke into a fit of coughing.

Annie rushed to his side and patted his back. "Pa, you need to rest."

"I'm fine," he insisted between coughs. "Just the dust."

Molly moved toward the door. "I should go. Eat the pies while they're still warm."

"Thank you," Annie said, meeting her friend's eyes. "Tell your mother we're grateful."

After Molly left, Annie helped her father sit down. "You need to go upstairs and lie down."

"There's too much work to do," he protested.

" Mr. Walter won't need his boots until Friday. I can finish them."

Her father looked at the piles of work that seemed to shrink each week. "What about the White boy's school shoes? And Mrs. Griffiths' walking boots need new heels."

"I'll get to them all," Annie promised. "But you need to rest if you want to get better."

After much grumbling, her father agreed to go upstairs to their living quarters above the shop. Annie helped him up the narrow stairs, one step at a time. His body felt lighter than it should, and his breathing came in short, sharp bursts that scared her.

Once in their small sitting room, she eased him into his chair.

"I'm not an old man yet," he protested.

"No, but you're a sick one," Annie said, keeping her voice light. "Now sit and rest while I make you some tea."

She moved to their tiny kitchen and put the kettle on the stove. While the water heated, she glanced at the letter that had arrived that morning. She'd hidden it under a book, but the edge still poked out, taunting her.

Her father's eyes were closed as she picked it up and read it again.

Final Notice: Three months' rent past due. Payment of £15 required within fourteen days or eviction proceedings will commence.

Annie folded the letter and tucked it into her pocket. Fifteen pounds. It might as well have been fifteen hundred for all their ability to pay it.

"What's that?" her father asked, opening his eyes.

"Nothing important," Annie lied. "Just a receipt."

While her father dozed in his chair, Annie returned to the shop. The meat pies sat untouched on the counter. She wrapped one carefully to save for her father's dinner and took a small bite of the other. The rich taste of meat and gravy made her stomach growl, reminding her she'd had nothing but a crust of bread since yesterday.

Through the window, she watched more people gather at the general store. Mr. Thompson had set up a display of the factory boots, and a crowd had formed to look at them. She recognized faces of people who had once been their customers.

She turned away and went back to Mr. Walter's boots, working until the stitches were perfect and the leather gleamed with polish. By the time the light began to fade, her back ached and her fingers were raw, but the boots looked as fine as any her father had ever made.

She lit the lamps and went upstairs to check on him. He was still in his chair, but awake now, staring out the window.

"I made some soup," she said, helping him to the table.

"Just broth again?" he asked, looking into the thin liquid.

"It's good for your chest," she said. "And there's a meat pie from Molly's mother."

His face brightened at that, and she felt a pang of guilt for the half-pie she'd already eaten.

"How's the work coming?" he asked between careful spoonful's.

"Mr. Walter's boots are done. I'll start on Mrs. Griffiths' tomorrow."

"Good, good." He nodded. "We need to keep our regular customers happy."

"Pa," Annie said, then paused. "How much money do we have left in the tin?"

His spoon stopped halfway to his mouth. "Why do you ask?"

"I just need to know."

He set the spoon down. "Not much. A few shillings, maybe a pound or two at most."

"And the rent is due," she said quietly.

"It can wait another week. Mr. Baxter has been our landlord for twenty years. He knows we're good for it."

Annie didn't mention the letter in her pocket or the fact that it wasn't Mr. Baxter sending it, but his son who had taken over the business and seemed far less patient than his father.

After dinner, she helped her father to bed, listening to the rattle in his chest as he breathed.

When she was sure he was asleep, she went back downstairs to the shop.

She opened the till and emptied the few coins onto the counter. Three shillings and sixpence. She added the coins from her own small purse...another two shillings she'd been saving for a new hair ribbon. Then she pulled out the old ledger from under the counter and opened it to the latest page.

The numbers told a story clearer than any words could. Six months ago, they'd had regular work and steady income. Now, week by week, the columns showed less money coming in and the same amount going out. The last entry showed a balance of three pounds, seven shillings.

Not enough for rent. Not even close.

Annie closed the ledger and rested her head in her hands. The shop had been her father's life, and before that, her grandfather's. The tools hanging on the walls had shaped leather for boots that had walked these streets for fifty years. And now it might all be lost because of machines in factories miles away that could stitch faster and cheaper than human hands.

A shadow passed by the window, and Annie looked up. Mrs. Wilson stood outside, peering in.

Annie quickly wiped her eyes and went to unlock the door.

"Mrs. Wilson? Is everything all right?"

The old woman stood in her worn coat, a pair of boots clutched to her chest. "I saw your light still on, child. I didn't want to disturb you so late."

"Come in, please. It's cold out there."

Mrs. Wilson stepped inside, the bell jingling softly. "I was hoping to ask about getting these fixed." She held out the boots. "The sole's coming loose, see? But I can wait until next week if you're busy."

Annie took the boots and examined them. The stitching had come undone along one side, and the leather was worn thin in places. "These need more than just a quick fix, Mrs. Wilson."

"Oh." The old woman's face fell. "I suppose they're not worth repairing then. I just thought..."

"No, no," Annie said quickly. "I can fix them. It's just, well, it will take some time and material."

"And how much will that cost?" Mrs. Wilson asked, her thin hands clutching her purse.

Annie remembered how Mrs. Wilson had sat with her for days after her mother died, bringing food and helping with washing and cleaning while Annie's father lost himself in grief.

"Nothing," Annie heard herself say. "Consider it payment for all you did for us when Ma passed."

"I can't let you do that," Mrs. Wilson protested. "Your father..."

"My father would agree," Annie said firmly. "I'll have them ready by Wednesday."

After Mrs. Wilson left, Annie turned the boots over in her hands. The leather for a new sole would cost at least a shilling, not to mention the thread and time. Money and materials they couldn't spare.

But some debts went beyond coins and notes. Some debts were paid in kindness.

Annie placed the boots on her workbench and turned down the lamps. Tomorrow would bring more work, more worry, and no doubt more people turning away from their door to buy cheap factory boots. But tonight, she would sleep knowing she'd done the right thing.

And perhaps that was worth more than all the rent money in the world.

TOM

The looms thundered like a hundred horses galloping across wooden floors. Tom Hartley guided the shuttle keeping his eyes on the threads that could snap and slice a finger clean off if a man wasn't careful. The mill air hung thick with cotton dust that caught in the throat and painted everything white, from the workers' hair to their lungs.

Five years at Harding's Textile Mill had taught Tom to breathe shallow and move quick. His hands had the memory now, and they could find the right thread even when his eyes watered from the dust.

"You stupid boy!" The shout cut through the machine noise, drawing Tom's attention to the far end of the floor.

Mr. Norris, the floor supervisor, stood over young Billy, red-faced and pointing at a tangle in the loom. Billy couldn't be more than sixteen, all skinny arms and frightened eyes. He'd only started two weeks ago after his father's accident in the loading bay.

"I'm sorry, sir," Billy stammered, trying to fix the jam. "The thread broke and I…"

"That's three yards of fabric ruined!" Norris grabbed Billy by the collar. "That comes out of your wages, boy!"

Tom secured his own loom and walked over. "Mr. Norris," he called. "That was my fault."

Norris turned, his grip still tight on Billy's shirt. "Your fault, Hartley? You weren't anywhere near this loom."

"I told Billy to watch mine while I stepped out," Tom lied smoothly. "He was trying to help me. If anyone loses wages, it should be me."

The supervisor's eyes narrowed. He knew Tom was lying—they both did—but Tom had been working the floor five years and knew how to fix problems that would take Norris hours to solve.

"Fine," Norris spat. "One shilling off your pay this week." He released Billy with a shove. "And you, watch what you're doing, or you'll be back on the streets where your pa will soon be."

After Norris stormed off, Billy turned to Tom with wide eyes. "You didn't have to do that."

"Get back to your loom before he changes his mind," Tom said, already turning to the tangled mess. "And watch how I fix this, so you'll know next time."

Billy hovered close as Tom worked to untangle the threads. "Will they really dock your pay a whole shilling?"

"Looks that way." Tom pulled a broken thread free. "Small price to pay for keeping that red-faced bull away from you."

"My ma can't afford for me to lose any pay," Billy said, his voice small. "Pa still can't walk after the accident, and the company doctor says he might not ever."

Tom nodded, thinking of the meager three shillings Billy would earn for a full week's work. Barely enough to feed one person, let alone a family. "You have brothers and sisters?"

"Three sisters. All younger."

The lunch whistle blew, a blessed relief from the noise and dust. Tom patted Billy's shoulder. "Bring your lunch outside. The air's a bit cleaner in the yard."

Outside, Tom found his usual spot against the brick wall. He unwrapped the cloth around his lunch. It was a chunk of bread, a small piece of cheese, and an apple his mother had insisted he take despite her own empty cupboards.

Billy joined him, unwrapping a much smaller bundle containing only a crust of bread.

"That's all you've got?" Tom asked.

Billy stared at the ground. "Ma says I'm a growing boy. I need to save the rest for my sisters."

Without a word, Tom broke his bread and cheese in half and handed them to Billy. "Take it."

"I can't…"

"You can and you will," Tom said firmly. "Man can't work these looms without food in his belly. You'll pass out face-first into the machine, and I'll have to explain to Mr. Norris why his newest worker lost his nose to a loom."

That got a small smile from Billy, who took the food with grateful hands. They ate in silence for a few minutes, watching other workers file into the yard.

"My pa went to see a man yesterday," Billy said suddenly. "A moneylender named Drake. Pa says he'll give us five pounds to keep us going until he can work again."

Tom stopped chewing. "Silas Drake?"

"You know him?"

"I know of him." Tom chose his words carefully. "Did your pa sign anything?"

"Some papers. Drake said it was just a formality. Interest is only a penny on the shilling per week."

Tom did the quick calculation. That was over twenty percent a month. No man working in a mill could ever pay that back.

"Tell your pa to be careful with Drake," Tom said. "Men like that, they don't lend money to be kind."

"Pa says he's got no choice. The mill owner won't give compensation for the accident, says it was Pa's fault for not watching where he stepped." Billy took a bite of cheese, savoring it. "What else can we do?"

Tom had no answer for that.

After their shift ended, Tom walked the three miles to his mother's small house on the edge of town. The road curved past the river where the water ran dark with dye from the mill, then up a gentle hill where squat worker cottages stood in tidy rows. His mother's home was one of the smallest, tucked at the end of the lane.

He knocked twice before using his key, finding

her at the table mending a shirt by the light of a single candle.

"Tom," she said, her face brightening. "I wasn't expecting you tonight."

"Thought I'd check on you," he said, bending to kiss her cheek. He set a small cloth bundle on the table. "Brought you some bread from Baker Street."

"You spoil me," she said, but her eyes lit up at the sight of the fresh loaf. "Sit down. I'll make tea."

"I'll make it," Tom insisted, taking the kettle to the stove. "How's your chest today?"

"Better than yesterday." She folded the shirt she'd been mending. "Mrs. Ainsley from church stopped by. Says her husband's shop might have some sewing work if I'm interested."

"That would be good." Tom didn't mention that Mr. Ainsley's tailor shop had been losing business to the new department store in town that sold ready-made clothes. One more craftsman being pushed out by factories and machines.

His mother seemed to read his thoughts. "I saw Mr. Sutherland in church on Sunday. Poor man could hardly make it up the steps, coughing so hard. His girl Annie had to help him the whole way."

"Harold Sutherland? The cobbler?"

"Mmm." She nodded. "Been sick most of the winter, they say. Annie runs the shop now, though I hear business isn't what it was. Those factory boots from London are half the price."

"Half the quality too, I bet," Tom said, pouring hot water into the teapot.

"Quality doesn't matter when a family has to choose between boots and bread." She accepted the cup he handed her. "Annie's a good girl. Devoted to her father. Reminds me of you in that way."

Tom felt his neck warm at the comparison. He knew Annie Sutherland by sight, a serious girl with auburn hair who rarely smiled these days. He'd passed her shop many times but had never had reason to go in. His own boots, while worn, still had life in them.

"Shame about their shop," he said, taking a seat across from his mother. "Craftsmen like Sutherland built this town before the mills came."

"And now the mills are pushing them out." His mother sipped her tea. "Mr. Baxter's son is threatening to evict them for back rent, Mrs. Wilson told me. Three months behind, she says."

Tom thought of his own wages, already stretched thin covering his room at the boarding house and helping his mother with her rent. "Times are hard for everyone."

"Harder for some than others." His mother reached across the table and patted his hand. "You're a good son, Tom Hartley. Your father would be proud of the man you've become."

They finished their tea in silence. Tom fixed a loose board on the front step before leaving, promising to visit again on Sunday.

The sky had darkened by the time he reached the Fox and Hound, a small pub favored by mill workers. The warmth and noise hit him as he opened the door, a welcome change from the chill spring evening. He spotted several familiar faces around the worn tables.

"Tom!" called Ned Porter, raising a mug in greeting. "Thought you weren't coming tonight."

"Had to see my mother first," Tom explained, sliding onto the bench beside Ned. "What did I miss?"

"Jack here was telling us about his cousin who lost his shop to Drake." Ned nodded toward Jack Davidson, an older worker with graying hair and missing fingers on his left hand, evidence of years working the dangerous machinery at the mill.

"Cousin had a butcher shop," Jack said, his voice

gruff from years of cotton dust. "Borrowed ten pounds from Drake when his wife took sick. Six months later, he owed thirty pounds and lost everything."

"How's that even possible?" asked another man, Frank Wiley, who worked in the boiler room.

"Drake's contracts," Jack said, tapping his temple. "Are full of words no working man can understand. Interest on interest, fees for this and that. By the time you realize what's happening, it's too late."

Tom thought of Billy's father and the five pounds he'd borrowed. "Can't the law do anything?"

Jack laughed without humor. "Law? Drake has the magistrate in his pocket. Man like that doesn't stay in business by playing fair."

Frank leaned in, lowering his voice. "You know Peters from the dye works? His brother-in-law couldn't pay Drake back. Next thing you know, his daughter's working in Drake's factory for no wages… just to pay off the debt. Fifteen hours a day, six days a week."

A chill ran through Tom that had nothing to do with the weather. "That can't be legal."

"Legal or not, it's happening," Jack said firmly. "And not just to Peters. Half a dozen men I know have borrowed from Drake in the last month alone."

"Times are hard," Ned agreed. "Mill's cutting wages again next month, I heard. And that new machine they installed does the work of three men."

"Three men who now have no work," Frank added grimly.

The conversation turned to other topics—the horse races, the new barmaid with the pretty smile, the preacher's Sunday sermon about the evils of drink delivered in a church half-filled with empty pews. Tom listened but said little, his mind on his own thin wallet.

His rent was due next week. His mother's the week after. The mill owner had already hinted at reduced hours for all but the most skilled workers. If he lost even a day's wages, he'd be short.

"You're quiet tonight, Tom," Ned observed.

"Just tired," Tom replied, draining his mug. "Think I'll head back."

"Speaking of Drake," Jack said as Tom stood, "saw him outside the cobbler's shop yesterday. The Sutherland's girl was talking to him."

Tom paused. "Annie Sutherland?"

Jack nodded. "Looked like he was offering help. The girl seemed to be considering it too."

"Can't blame her," Frank said with a shrug.

"Shop's been empty for weeks, and her pa's too sick to work. Girl's got to eat."

Tom thought of Annie's serious face and proud posture. The idea of her at Drake's mercy twisted something in his gut.

"Good night, lads," he said, dropping a few coins on the table. "Early start tomorrow."

The walk back to his boarding house gave Tom time to think. His own savings had dwindled to less than a pound. Not enough to help his mother if her rent increased again, let alone a stranger like Annie Sutherland.

But the thought of her signing one of Drake's contracts, not understanding the trap until it was too late, stayed with him all the way home.

Three streets away from his boarding house, he passed the cobbler's shop. A single light burned in the window. Seems Annie was still awake, perhaps working by candlelight to save what her father had built.

Tom paused, looking at the light. What could one mill worker do against men like Drake? Not much, perhaps.

But his father had taught him that when you see someone drowning, you don't ask if they can swim. You jump in and help them reach the shore.

With that thought, Tom continued home, already forming a plan in his mind. There might be a way to help Annie Sutherland without wounding her pride or emptying his own pockets.

All it would take was a pair of boots in need of repair.

ANNIE

"What do you mean you can't extend any more credit, Mr. Finch? I've been coming to this tannery since I was a child."

Annie stood in the dim workroom of Finch's Tannery, the smell of chemicals and cured hides filling her nose. The morning light barely filtered through the grimy windows, casting shadows over piles of leather and tools.

Mr. Finch wiped his hands on his apron and shook his head. "I'm sorry, Annie. Your father has always been good for his debts, but it's been three months now. I have my own bills to pay."

"I can give you a pound now," Annie said, pulling the precious coin from her pocket. It was meant for the landlord, but she needed materials more urgently than she needed another week of grace. "And the rest when we finish Mr. Walter's order."

"A pound?" Mr. Finch frowned. "You owe five pounds, seven shillings. The best leather costs money, Annie. I can't run my business on promises."

"Then I'll take scraps," Annie said, trying to keep the desperation from her voice. "Whatever you can spare for a pound."

Mr. Finch's face softened. He'd known her since she was small enough to hide behind her father's legs. "Let me see what I can find."

He disappeared into the back room, leaving Annie alone with her thoughts. The tannery had supplied her father's shop for twenty years. Her grandfather before that. Now she stood here like a beggar, asking for scraps.

When Mr. Finch returned, he carried a small bundle wrapped in paper. "This is what I can give you for a pound. Some offcuts from the Carter order and a few bits of sole leather. Not enough for boots, but you might get some repairs out of it."

Annie took the bundle, fighting to keep her expression neutral. "Thank you."

"Annie," Mr. Finch called as she turned to leave. "If things are that bad, perhaps it's time to consider other work. My wife knows a family looking for a maid. Good people, fair wages."

Annie felt heat rise in her face. "We're not that desperate yet, Mr. Finch."

"There's no shame in honest work, girl."

"And what my father and I do isn't honest work?" She regretted the words as soon as they left her mouth.

Mr. Finch sighed. "You know that's not what I meant."

"I know. I'm sorry." Annie tucked the bundle under her arm. "Thank you for these."

Outside, the morning air was crisp, the streets beginning to fill with workers heading to factories and shops. Annie clutched her purchase, mentally sorting through what little she might make with such poor materials. Perhaps she could cobble together enough for Mrs. Wilson's boots repair, but not much else.

She was so lost that she didn't notice the man rushing around the corner until they collided. The impact knocked her backward, sending her bundle flying from her arms. Its contents scattered across the wet cobblestones.

"I'm so sorry!" A man dropped to his knees in front of her, scrambling to gather her leather pieces from the mud. "My fault entirely. Wasn't looking where I was going."

Annie knelt to snatch her supplies before they were ruined by the mud and horse droppings that littered the street. "You should watch where you're walking," she snapped.

"You're right, and I'm sorry." The man looked up at her with an apologetic smile. He had dark hair that fell across his forehead and a face that seemed made for smiling. Something about him was familiar. "I'm late for my shift at the mill."

"Well, now you've made me late too," Annie said, grabbing a piece of leather from a puddle. She could have cried at the sight of the water seeping into the material. That was Mr. Walter's heel patch ruined.

"Here, let me help you." The man gathered the remaining pieces and handed them to her. "I'm Tom. Tom Hartley."

Annie finally placed him. He was a mill worker who sometimes sat three pews back at church. She'd noticed him once or twice helping his mother up the steps, much as she did with her father.

"I don't need help," she said, shoving the leather back into the wrapping. "I need people to look where they're going."

"Fair enough." Tom smiled again, seemingly

untroubled by her coldness. "Are you Miss Sutherland? From the cobbler shop?"

Annie nodded curtly, checking to make sure she had everything. "I need to go."

"Wait." Tom reached for something beneath a cart. "You dropped this."

He held out a small leather-working tool, an awl her father had made specially for her smaller hands. The handle was worn smooth from years of use, the metal polished from constant handling.

"Thank you," she said, taking it quickly.

"I think something might have fallen in here too." Tom peered under the cart. "Let me check."

"I have everything," Annie insisted, stepping back. "Good day, Mr. Hartley."

She hurried away, feeling his eyes on her back. Only when she turned the corner did she allow herself to examine the damage. The leather was muddied, some pieces soaked through. The pound she'd spent—a pound she couldn't spare—had bought her little more than ruined scraps.

Back at the shop, Annie spread the leather on her workbench and tried to salvage what she could. Most pieces were still usable with some cleaning, but the quality was poor even before the mud. Patches and offcuts of inconsistent thickness. Nothing like the materials they'd once used.

The bell above the door jingled, and Annie looked up, hoping for a customer. Instead, Tom Hartley stood in the doorway, cap in hand.

"Miss Sutherland," he said, stepping inside. "I wanted to make sure you got home all right."

Annie stared at him. "As you can see, I did."

"I also wanted to return this." He held out a small leather punch. "It was under the cart. Must have rolled there when you dropped your things."

Annie hadn't even noticed it was missing. She reached for it, careful not to touch his fingers. "Thank you."

Tom's eyes moved around the shop, taking in the empty racks that once held rows of boots and shoes. The workbenches with half-finished repairs. The layer of dust on surfaces that had once been polished daily.

"I'd like to pay for any damage," he said. "To your materials."

Annie felt shame twist in her stomach. She didn't need his pity. "The damage is minimal."

"Even so, it was my fault." Tom reached into his pocket and placed a few coins on the counter. "I insist."

"Take your money," Annie said, pushing the coins back toward him. "We don't need charity."

"It's not charity. It's making things right." His voice remained calm, friendly even, which only irritated her more.

"Mr. Hartley, I appreciate your concern, but I have work to do." Annie turned back to her bench, a clear dismissal.

Instead of leaving, Tom approached her workbench. "What are you making?"

"Repairs for Mrs. Wilson's boots," Annie said, hoping her short answers would drive him away.

"You know, my mother speaks highly of your father's work," Tom said. "Says he made the best boots in the county."

"He still does," Annie corrected. "When he's well."

"Of course." Tom nodded. "I didn't mean to suggest otherwise."

An awkward silence fell between them. Annie continued cleaning mud from a piece of leather, intensely aware of Tom watching her hands work.

"Well," he said finally, "I won't keep you from your work." He moved toward the door but paused with his hand on the knob. "If you ever need anything, Miss Sutherland, my mother and I would be happy to help."

"We're managing fine," Annie said, not looking up.

"I'm sure you are." Tom smiled again, that easy smile that suggested life was full of simple solutions. "Good day, Miss Sutherland."

Only when the door closed behind him did Annie release the breath she'd been holding. Who did he think he was, offering help like she was some charity case? And why was he so determined to be friendly?

She picked up the coins he'd left, intending to return them the next time she saw him. Three shillings, more than fair for the minimal damage, but she couldn't bring herself to keep them. Pride was sometimes all a person had left.

The day dragged on with no customers. Annie finished Mrs. Wilson's boots, then started on Mrs. Griffiths walking shoes, though she doubted the woman would return for them. The shop felt too quiet without her father's humming or the tap of his hammer.

Mid-afternoon, she went upstairs to check on him. She found him sitting up in bed, paper and pencil in hand.

"What are you doing, Pa?" she asked, setting down the cup of tea she'd brought him.

"Drawing a new boot pattern," he said, his voice

raspy. "Thought we might try something different. Compete with those factory models."

Annie smiled, hiding her concern at how thin his face had become. "That's a good idea."

"How was Finch? Did he give you credit for the order?"

Annie hesitated. "Not exactly. But I got enough for the repairs we have."

Her father's face fell. "I see."

"It's fine, Pa. We'll manage."

He shook his head. "I should be down there helping you. Not lying here like an invalid while you do everything."

"You need to rest to get better," Annie said firmly. "Doctor Perkins said so."

At the mention of the doctor, her father frowned. "We can't afford another visit from him."

"Let me worry about that." Annie helped him sit up straighter against his pillows. "Now, tell me about this new design."

Her father spent the next hour describing his idea for boots that combined the comfort of handmade with the lower cost of factory models. His eyes lit up as he talked, reminding Annie of how he used to be before the illness - full of energy and ideas.

A knock at the door interrupted them. Annie

went downstairs to find Doctor Perkins on the step, medical bag in hand.

"Good afternoon, Miss Sutherland," he said, stepping inside. "I was passing and thought I'd check on your father."

Annie knew this wasn't true. The doctor never "passed by" without being called. Someone had sent him, and that meant someone would pay his fee.

"He's upstairs," she said, leading the way. "His cough seems worse today."

Doctor Perkins examined her father thoroughly, listening to his chest and asking about his symptoms. Annie watched from the doorway, noting the doctor's frown as he heard the rattle in her father's lungs.

"The congestion is still there, Mr. Sutherland," the doctor said, packing away his stethoscope. "I'm going to prescribe a stronger tonic for that cough. And you need complete rest. No work at all for at least two weeks."

Her father started to protest, but a coughing fit cut him off. When he could speak again, he asked, "And how much will this tonic cost, Doctor?"

"Don't worry about that now," Doctor Perkins said. "Let's focus on getting you well."

He motioned for Annie to follow him downstairs. In the shop, he wrote out a prescription and handed it to her.

"He needs this tonic twice daily," the doctor explained. "And beef broth if you can manage it. His body needs strength to fight off the infection."

Annie looked at the prescription, recognizing the name of an expensive medicine sold at Phillips' Pharmacy. "How much will this cost?"

"Three shillings for the bottle," Doctor Perkins said. "But it should last a week if you're careful with the dosing."

Three shillings, exactly what Tom Hartley had left on her counter. Annie felt her stomach sink.

"I'll get it today," she promised.

The doctor hesitated, then said, "You know, it's curious. A young man stopped by my office this morning asking about your father's condition."

Annie stiffened. "What young man?"

"Tom Hartley, from the mill. He said he was a friend of the family." Doctor Perkins gave her a questioning look. "He seemed quite concerned."

"He's not a friend," Annie said quickly. "Just someone we know from church."

"Well, friend or not, he left something for your father's care." The doctor reached into his pocket and pulled out a small envelope. "He insisted it was repayment of a debt to your father, but I thought you should know."

Annie stared at the envelope, unable to speak. She didn't need to open it to know what was inside, money for the doctor's visit and probably for the medicine too.

"I can't accept this," she said finally.

"Mr. Hartley was quite adamant," Doctor Perkins said. "Your father once made boots for him at a reduced price when he couldn't afford the full cost. He considered this settling an old debt."

Annie knew this was a lie. Her father kept meticulous records of all transactions, and he had never mentioned Tom Hartley. This was charity, plain and simple.

"Miss Sutherland," the doctor said gently, "I've known your family a long time. Your father would want you to accept help when it's offered in good faith."

"My father would want to pay his own way," Annie insisted.

"Perhaps." Doctor Perkins placed the envelope on the counter. "But he would want you to do whatever is necessary to keep this shop open and food on your table. Pride can't cure illness, Annie."

With that, he picked up his bag and headed for

the door. "Make sure he takes that tonic. I'll check back next week."

After the doctor left, Annie stood staring at the envelope. Part of her wanted to run after him and return it. Another part, the practical part that had kept them afloat these past months, knew they needed the help.

She picked up the envelope and opened it. Inside were ten shillings and it would be enough for the medicine and the doctor's visit, with a little left over for food. Ten shillings that Tom Hartley, a mill worker with his own mother to support, had given them.

Why would he do such a thing? They weren't friends. Barely acquaintances. Yet he'd gone out of his way to help them, inventing a debt to spare her pride.

Annie slipped the money into her pocket, a confusing mix of emotions swirling inside her. Gratitude at the help they desperately needed. Suspicion of Tom's motives. Shame at having to accept charity. And beneath it all, a small spark of something that felt dangerously like hope.

She would use the money for her father's medicine. She had no choice. But she would find a way to repay Tom Hartley, whether he wanted repayment or not. She was a Sutherland, after all, and Sutherlands always paid their debts.

Even as she thought this, a small voice whispered that perhaps Tom's kindness wasn't about money at all. Perhaps he truly cared about her father's well-being. About her well-being.

She pushed the thought away and went upstairs to tell her father about the new medicine. Some things were better left unexamined in the harsh light of their circumstances. And Tom Hartley's inexplicable kindness was certainly one of them.

TOM

"Hartley! Mind that shuttle or you'll lose your fingers!"

Tom snapped his attention back to the loom as Mr. Norris shouted from across the workshop floor. The cotton threads had begun to tangle where his hands had slowed, distracted by thoughts that had nothing to do with textile work.

"Sorry, sir," Tom called back, quickly correcting the problem before it could jam the machine.

The thundering noise of the mill swallowed Norris's grumbled response. Tom wiped sweat from his brow and focused on the rhythm of the shuttle, back and forth, back and forth, trying to push away the memory of Annie Sutherland's face when she'd discovered he'd paid toward her father's medical bills.

Pride. That's what he'd seen in her eyes. Not gratitude. And suspicion, as if kindness must always hide selfish motives.

For the next hour, Tom worked, his hands moving with the skill that had kept him employed while other men were replaced by newer machines. But his mind kept wandering to the cobbler's shop and the young woman who seemed determined to carry her burdens alone.

When the lunch whistle blew, Tom collected his bundle and headed to the yard. He spotted Jack Davidson sitting on his usual crate, eating bread and cheese with slow, deliberate bites. At fifty-eight, Jack was one of the oldest workers at the mill, respected for his knowledge and feared for his blunt opinions.

"Mind if I join you?" Tom asked, approaching the older man.

Jack moved his coat to make space on the crate. "Free country, ain't it?"

Tom sat and unwrapped his lunch. A bread and a small chunk of ham his mother had made. "Jack, you know everyone in town. What do you know about the Sutherlands? The cobbler family."

Jack glanced at Tom with interest. "Harold

Sutherland? Known him thirty years or more. Why do you ask?"

"Just curious," Tom said, tearing his bread in half. "Heard he's been ill."

"Lung fever, from what they say." Jack nodded. "Bad business, that. There was a time when Harold Sutherland was the finest bootmaker in three counties. Folk from Manchester would travel here just to have him fit them. Even Governor once ordered a pair."

"That good?"

"Better." Jack held up his hand, displaying the two missing fingers. "After this happened, I couldn't get boots to fit right. Everything rubbed blisters or pinched. Harold studied my walk, measured both feet ten different ways, and made boots so perfect I forgot I was wearing them." He shook his head. "Man's a craftsman in the true sense of the word."

"What about his daughter? Annie?"

Jack's eyebrows rose. "Annie? She practically grew up in that shop. Could thread a needle before most girls could tie their pinafores. When her mother died, must be ten years now, she stepped right in. Does most of the work these days with Harold laid up."

"Her mother died?" Tom asked, surprised. He hadn't known that.

"Fever took her. Annie was just a girl, fourteen or fifteen maybe." Jack took a drink from his tin cup. "Harold was never the same after that. Threw himself into his work, kept Annie close. Folk say he refused three offers for her hand already."

"Three?" Tom tried to sound merely interested rather than surprised.

"Baker's son for one. Then a clerk from the bank." Jack shrugged. "Third was Dixon from the iron works. Harold turned them all away, said Annie was too young. Truth is, I think he couldn't bear to lose her too."

"And now with Harold sick..."

"The shop's failing," Jack said matter-of-factly. "Those factory boots are killing craftsmen like Sutherland. Half the price, quarter the quality, but folk can't afford better these days." He eyed Tom curiously. "Why all the questions about the Sutherlands?"

"I saw Annie at Finch's tannery yesterday morning," Tom said, offering a partial truth. "She seemed troubled."

"Wouldn't you be? Trying to keep a dying business afloat while nursing a sick father?" Jack shook his head. "Pride's the trouble there. Sutherlands never liked taking help. Harold would rather starve than admit he needs a hand."

"And Annie takes after him?"

"Cut from the same cloth, those two." Jack finished his lunch and dusted crumbs from his shirt.

The lunch whistle blew again, signaling the end of their break. As they walked back to their looms, Jack placed a hand on Tom's arm.

"Whatever you're thinking of doing, be careful," he warned. "Sutherland pride cuts both ways. Help them wrong, and you'll make things worse."

Tom nodded, Jack's words echoing in his mind as he returned to work. For the rest of his shift, he worked steadily, forming a plan. If Annie wouldn't accept charity, perhaps she would accept honest business.

When the end-of-day whistle blew, Tom collected his pay, docked one shilling as Norris had threatened, and headed not toward his boarding house but to the cobbler's shop on High Street.

The shop bell jingled as he entered. Annie stood at the workbench, head bent over a pair of women's boots. She looked up, her expression changing from hope to wariness when she saw him.

"Mr. Hartley," she said, setting down her tools. "What can I do for you?"

Tom removed his cap. "I need boot repairs, Miss Sutherland. Wondered if you might help."

Suspicion flickered across her face. "Let me see them."

Tom sat on the small bench and removed his right boot, then his left. They were indeed worn. The sole of the right beginning to separate, the heel of the left worn down unevenly from his walk.

Annie took them, her fingers moving over the leather with practiced ease. "Factory made," she said, a hint of disdain in her voice.

"Best I could afford three years ago," Tom admitted. "But they've served me well."

She continued her examination, turning the boots over in her hands. "The leather's decent quality. Worth repairing." She looked up at him. "This will cost you."

"I expected so." Tom smiled. "What's your price?"

Annie hesitated, and Tom could almost see her weighing what he might be able to pay against what the work was truly worth, perhaps considering charging extra given his earlier interference with the doctor.

"Five shillings," she said finally. "For both boots.

New heels, the right sole restitched, and I'll oil the leather to preserve it."

It was a fair price, perhaps even slightly less than what the work was worth. Tom nodded. "When can I collect them?"

"Friday." Annie wrote the order in a leather-bound book. "I'll need two shillings now, the rest on collection."

Tom counted out the coins and placed them on the counter. "Thank you, Miss Sutherland."

As she wrote him a receipt, Tom glanced around the shop. He noticed details he'd missed on his previous visit, the quality of the tools hanging on the wall, the precise organization of materials, the half-finished pair of children's shoes that showed craftsmanship factory boots could never match.

"Your father taught you well," he said.

Annie looked up, startled. "What?"

"Your work," Tom clarified, nodding toward the children's shoes. "The stitching is perfect."

A flush of color touched Annie's cheeks, though whether from pride or embarrassment, Tom couldn't tell. "Pa says hands remember what minds forget. I've been stitching leather since I was six years old."

"It shows." Tom accepted the receipt she handed

him. "My mother always said you can tell a true craftsman by how they handle their tools. Like they're part of their hands."

Annie's expression softened slightly. "Your mother sounds like a wise woman."

"She is." Tom smiled. "Though she'd say she's just old."

Almost against her will, Annie's lips curved in the ghost of a smile. Tom counted that as a victory.

"Will you need other boots while these are being repaired?" she asked, business-like once more.

"I have an old pair that'll do for a few days." Tom moved toward the door. "Friday, then?"

Annie nodded. "Friday."

As he turned to leave, his eyes caught on a small envelope on the counter, the same envelope he'd left with Doctor Perkins. He paused, then decided not to mention it. Let her have her pride.

"Good evening, Miss Sutherland," he said instead.

"Mr. Hartley," she called as he reached for the door handle. He turned back. "About the doctor's visit..."

Tom waited, watching emotions play across her face.

"Thank you," she said finally, the words sounding

as if they'd been pulled from deep within her. "But I can't accept…"

"It's not charity," Tom interrupted gently. "It's what neighbors do. We help each other when times are hard."

"Even so, I'll repay you," Annie insisted. "Every penny."

Tom knew better than to argue. "As you wish, Miss Sutherland."

"Annie," she said, then looked surprised at herself. "My name is Annie."

"Annie," Tom repeated, smiling. "I'm Tom."

Her nod was almost imperceptible. "Good evening, Tom."

"Good evening, Annie."

ANNIE

"*Final notice: Payment in full of fifteen pounds required within seven days or eviction proceedings will commence...*"

Annie folded the letter and pressed it flat on the counter, as if the physical act could somehow flatten the fear swelling in her chest. A week. They had a week to find fifteen pounds, money they simply didn't have.

She glanced upstairs where her father slept, his breathing still raspy despite the medicine Tom Hartley had paid for. That medicine would run out soon, and the doctor would need to be paid for his next visit.

Her gaze fell on the ledger. It was open with its neat columns showing more going out than coming in. Three repaired pairs of boots waited for customers who might never return. The leather from Finch's was nearly gone. And now this notice again, with its cold, final words.

Annie gathered her shawl and the letter. She had avoided this moment for months, had told herself there would always be another way. But the walls were closing in, and pride wouldn't keep a roof over their heads.

The banking house stood on Market Street, a gray stone building with polished brass fixtures and heavy oak doors. Annie hesitated on the steps, her reflection wavering in the glass panels. Her dress was clean but faded, her hair pulled back in a simple knot. She looked exactly what she was, a tradesman's daughter coming to beg.

Inside, the marble floor echoed with each step. A clerk looked up from his high desk, eyes moving over Annie.

"May I help you?" he asked, his voice as stiff as his collar.

"I wish to speak with Mr. Drake," Annie said, proud that her voice didn't shake.

The clerk's eyebrows rose slightly. "Do you have an appointment?"

"No, but…"

"Mr. Drake sees clients by appointment only." He returned to his ledger, dismissing her.

Annie stood her ground. "Please tell Mr. Drake that Miss Sutherland from the cobbler shop on High Street wishes to discuss a business matter."

The clerk sighed but rose from his desk. "Wait here."

He disappeared through a door, leaving Annie standing in the high-ceilinged room. Other clients, all men in suits far finer than anything her father had owned even in better days, sat in leather chairs, reading newspapers or speaking in low voices about investments and trades. None looked at her directly, but she felt their awareness of her presence, an intruder in their domain.

Minutes stretched into an hour, then two. The clerk returned several times to usher other clients through the polished door, but never Annie. She remained standing, refusing to sit though her feet ached. If this was meant to humble her, she would not show it.

The clock on the wall struck three when the clerk finally approached again.

"Mr. Drake will see you now," he said, as if he hadn't kept her waiting half the day.

He led her down a corridor to a door at the end, knocking once before opening it.

"Miss Sutherland, sir."

The room beyond was wood-paneled and lined with bookshelves. A large desk dominated the space, behind which sat a man in his forties with salt-and-pepper hair and a precisely trimmed beard. He didn't rise as Annie entered.

"Miss Sutherland," Silas Drake said, his voice smooth as polished stone. "Please, sit."

Annie sat in the chair across from his desk, placing her shawl in her lap. "Thank you for seeing me, Mr. Drake."

"I make it a point to know every business in town," Drake said, leaning back in his chair. "Your father runs the cobbler shop on High Street. Or rather, you do now, with his illness."

Annie wasn't surprised he knew this. Drake's business was knowing who needed money and why.

"Yes," she said. "Our shop has been there for thirty years."

"A respectable establishment," Drake agreed. "Though I understand business has been...difficult of late."

There was no point in pretense. "We've fallen

behind on our rent. Three months. The landlord has given us one week to pay in full or face eviction."

Drake's expression didn't change. "Fifteen pounds, I believe?"

Again, Annie wasn't surprised he knew the exact amount. "Yes."

"A substantial sum for a small shop." Drake opened a drawer and removed a ledger. "Especially with your father unable to work and those factory boots taking your business."

Annie felt a flush of anger at his casual assessment of their situation but kept her voice steady. "It's why I've come to you. We need a loan."

Drake made a note in his ledger. "I see. And what collateral do you offer?"

"Collateral?"

"Something of value to secure the loan," he explained, as if to a child. "Property, valuables, that sort of thing."

Annie's hands tightened in her lap. "We have the tools of our trade. Some leather stock. Our furniture."

Drake made another note. "Used cobbler's tools and worn furniture. Not much security there, Miss Sutherland."

"Our shop has a reputation," Annie insisted. "We have loyal customers."

"Not enough to pay your rent, it seems." Drake closed his ledger. "However, I might be persuaded to help. Seven pounds now to cover part of your debt and provide working capital. The rest we can discuss...arrangements for."

Annie frowned. "Seven pounds? But I need fifteen."

"Seven pounds is what I'm prepared to offer today." Drake's voice remained pleasant. "Perhaps more later, when I see how...responsible you are with this first amount."

Something in his tone made Annie uncomfortable, but she pressed on. "And the terms?"

"Standard," Drake said with a wave of his hand. "One penny on the shilling per week. Simple interest, nothing complex."

Annie did the calculation quickly. "That's more than twenty percent a month."

Drake smiled. "You're quick with figures. A valuable skill in business."

"It's too high," Annie said. "We'll never be able to repay at that rate."

"Then perhaps we could come to an... alternate arrangement." Drake's eyes moved over her face, down to her hands, and back up. "I have several enterprises that require skilled workers. Your hands look quite capable."

Annie felt a chill at his assessment. "I'm needed at our shop."

"Of course, of course." Drake leaned forward. "Well, Miss Sutherland, those are my terms. Seven pounds now at the stated interest. I have the paperwork here if you wish to proceed."

Annie hesitated. Everything inside her warned against this, but the image of her father being thrown into the street, his tools confiscated, their home lost, that was unthinkable.

"I'll need to discuss this with my father," she said.

"Family consultation. Admirable." Drake nodded. "But do remember your deadline. The landlord won't wait, and neither will I. This offer stands for today only."

Annie stood, gathering her shawl. "I'll return tomorrow with my answer."

"I look forward to it." Drake rose at last, extending his hand across the desk. "Your father built a fine reputation in this town, Miss Sutherland. It would be a shame to see it end."

His hand was dry and cold, his grip too firm and

too long. Annie withdrew hers as soon as politeness allowed.

Outside, the afternoon had turned gray, clouds gathering for rain. Annie walked quickly, turning Drake's offer over in her mind. Five pounds wouldn't solve their problem, only delay it. And that interest rate would ensure they never escaped the debt.

But what choice did they have?

The shop bell jingled as Annie entered, and she was surprised to find someone waiting inside. Molly Peters stood by the counter, a bundle wrapped in brown paper under her arm.

"Annie!" Molly smiled. "I've been waiting ages. Where have you been?"

"Business," Annie said, unwilling to explain. "Is something wrong?"

"Wrong? No!" Molly placed her bundle on the counter. "I brought you these. Mrs. Davis was clearing out the sewing room and found all these leather scraps from when we made those purses last summer."

She unwrapped the package to reveal a stack of leather pieces, small but good quality, in browns and blacks with a few pieces of deep green and burgundy.

"They're not much," Molly admitted. "But I thought you might use them for patches or trim."

Annie ran her fingers over the leather, emotion tightening her throat. "Thank you, Molly. This is...this helps."

"There's something else too," Molly lowered her voice though they were alone. "I heard some of the men at the mill talking about needing boot repairs. I may have mentioned that I knew the best cobbler in town."

"You didn't," Annie said.

"I did," Molly grinned. "And three of them asked where your shop was. I told them you do the finest repairs for half what new boots cost."

For the first time that day, Annie felt a spark of hope. "Molly Peters, you're an angel."

"I know," Molly said with mock seriousness. "That's why I expect a discount when I need new shoes." Her expression grew concerned. "Annie, you look tired. Are you all right?"

Annie considered deflecting the question as she always did, insisting she was fine. But everything suddenly felt too heavy to carry alone.

"No," she admitted. "I'm not all right."

Molly immediately moved to her side. "What is it? Is it your father?"

"Partly." Annie sank onto the bench, Molly beside her. "The landlord has given us one week to pay three months' back rent. Fifteen pounds."

"Fifteen pounds!" Molly gasped. "Annie, that's…"

"Money we don't have," Annie finished. "I know."

"What will you do?"

Annie looked down at her hands. "I went to see Silas Drake today."

Molly's face paled. "Oh, Annie, no."

"He offered Seven pounds," Annie continued. "At one penny on the shilling per week."

"That's highway robbery," Molly said, indignant. "And not nearly enough besides."

"It would buy us time to find the rest," Annie reasoned. "With new customers from the mill, perhaps…"

"Annie, listen to me." Molly took her hands. "My cousin Eliza borrowed from Drake last year when her husband died. She couldn't keep up with the payments, and Drake offered her 'work' to pay off the debt."

"What kind of work?"

"In his factory at first. Sixteen hours a day, six days a week. The wages never seemed to reduce the debt." Molly's voice dropped further. "When she complained, they moved her to one of his other...businesses."

Annie frowned. "What do you mean?"

"He owns buildings down by the docks," Molly said delicately. "Where men go at night."

Understanding dawned, and Annie felt sick. "Surely he couldn't force her."

"Not directly. But when you owe a man like Drake and have children to feed, what choice is there?"

Annie thought of Drake's cold eyes assessing her. His comment about her "capable hands."

"I had no idea," she said.

"Few do, until it's too late." Molly squeezed her hands. "Promise me you won't sign anything with him, Annie. We'll find another way."

"What other way? The poor box at church? Charity?"

"If necessary, yes," Molly insisted. "Better that than Drake."

Annie stood and moved to the counter, straightening tools that didn't need straightening. "I won't accept charity, Molly. My father built this business. I won't be the one to lose it."

"Stubbornness won't save it either," Molly said gently. "Sometimes we need help."

Annie thought of Tom Hartley, of the money he'd left for the doctor. He'd called it "what neighbors do," but it was charity all the same.

"I'll think about what you've said," Annie promised. "No decisions today."

Mollified, Molly gathered her shawl. "Good. And I'll ask around about work. Mrs. Davis mentioned the mayor's wife needs new walking boots. I'll make sure she knows about your shop."

After Molly left, Annie climbed the stairs to check on her father. He was awake, sitting up in bed with one of his pattern books.

"There you are," he said, voice still raspy. "I thought I heard voices."

"Molly stopped by," Annie said, pouring him a cup of water. "She brought some leather scraps from the sewing room."

"That was kind." He took the cup with shaking hands. "Any customers today?"

Annie hesitated, then decided against mentioning the eviction notice or Drake. "Not yet. But Molly said some men from the mill might come for repairs."

"Good, good." He studied her face. "You look troubled, girl. What is it?"

"Nothing, Pa. Just tired."

He didn't believe her, she could see that, but he didn't press. "You work too hard, Annie. You should be out with friends, meeting young men, thinking about your own home someday."

"I am home," Annie said firmly. "Right where I want to be."

Her father's eyes grew damp. "You're a good daughter. Better than I deserve."

"Don't talk nonsense," Annie chided gently. "Now rest. I need to run to the church before evening service."

Outside, the sky had darkened further, and a fine drizzle had begun to fall. Annie pulled her shawl over her head and hurried through the streets toward St. Mark's Church.

The church was empty except for Reverend Clarke, who stood at the altar counting coins from the poor box into neat piles.

"Miss Sutherland," he called as she entered. "Come in out of the rain."

Annie moved up the aisle, her footsteps echoing in the empty space. "Good evening, Reverend. I hope I'm not disturbing you."

"Not at all." He smiled, his kind face lined with years of both joy and sorrow shared with his congregation. "What brings you out in this weather?"

Annie twisted her damp shawl in her hands. "I wanted to ask about...about the poor box."

Understanding filled the reverend's eyes. "Ah. Things are difficult at the shop?"

"Yes," Annie admitted. "We've fallen behind on our rent. The landlord has given us a week."

Reverend Clarke looked down at the meager piles of coins before him. "I wish I could help, Annie. Truly I do. But we had that terrible accident at the Preston mine last week. Three families left without fathers. Every penny we've collected is promised to them for food and coal."

Annie had known this would be the answer, but disappointment still stung. "Of course. Those families need it more than we do."

"How much do you need?" the reverend asked.

"Fifteen pounds," Annie said, the sum sounding even more impossible when spoken aloud.

Reverend Clarke shook his head sadly. "Even in better times, our box rarely sees more than two or three pounds a month."

"I understand," Annie said. "I shouldn't have asked."

"Never be ashamed to ask for help, child," the reverend said gently. "God works through many hands."

"But not this time, it seems," Annie said, unable to keep the bitterness from her voice.

"Perhaps not through mine," Reverend Clarke agreed. "But that doesn't mean help won't come. Have faith, Annie."

Faith. Annie had had faith when her mother was dying, praying through the night as fever ravaged her body. She'd had faith when the first factory boots arrived in town, believing quality would win out over price. Faith had brought her little comfort and less relief.

"Thank you for your time, Reverend," she said, turning to leave.

"Annie," he called after her. "I'll speak to some of the parish council. Perhaps we can find temporary lodgings if the worst happens."

The worst. Being evicted. Losing their home, the shop, everything her father had built. Annie couldn't bear to consider it.

"I appreciate that," she said, though they both knew she would never accept such help.

Outside, the drizzle had turned to rain. Annie pulled her shawl tighter and began the walk home, her mind churning with limited options. Drake's offer now seemed both more necessary and more dangerous. Molly's warning echoed in her head, but so did the landlord's deadline.

Lost in thought, she didn't notice the figure approaching until they were nearly face to face. Tom Hartley stood under the shelter of a shop awning, a package under his arm. For a moment, they stared at each other through the rain. his face concerned, hers guarded.

She should say something. Thank him again for the doctor's money. Ask about his boots. Anything.

But something locked her voice in her throat. Instead, she nodded once, then hurried past, feeling his eyes follow her down the street.

Only when she turned the corner did she slow her pace, berating herself for her foolishness. Tom had shown her nothing but kindness. He deserved at least basic courtesy in return.

But kindness created obligation, and Annie had obligations enough already.

She wiped rain from her face, telling herself it was only water and not tears of frustration. Tomorrow she would have to decide about Drake's offer. Tomorrow she would have to find a way forward, with or without help.

Tonight, though, she would check on her father,

repair Mrs. Wilson's boots, and pretend, just for a few hours, that things might somehow work out.

Through the rain, the cobbler shop sign appeared ahead. Annie squared her shoulders and lifted her chin. Whatever came, she would face it as a Sutherland: with skilled hands, a clear eye, and yes, with pride intact.

Even if that pride cost her everything.

TOM

"You want to work the boiler room night shift? Are you mad, Hartley?"

Tom stood in the small, cluttered office of Mr. Grant, the mill foreman. The walls were covered with production schedules, time sheets, and stern notices about safety protocols that the mill management routinely ignored.

"I need the money, Mr. Grant," Tom said. "The night shift pays three shillings more per week."

"Three shillings more because most men with sense won't take it." Grant leaned back in his chair, which creaked under his weight. "You're one of my best loom workers. Why throw that away for the boiler room?"

"I'm not throwing anything away. I'll still work my regular shift."

Grant's eyebrows shot up. "Both shifts? Sixteen hours a day?"

"Just until I can set aside enough for my mother's rent. A month, maybe two."

"A month in that boiler room is enough to kill a man." Grant shook his head. "Heat like the devil's own kitchen. Coal dust so thick you can write your name in what you cough up after a shift. Men collapse regular from exhaustion."

Tom had heard the stories. Everyone had. The boiler room that powered the mill's steam engines was the most dangerous place in the factory, not from sudden accidents like the looms could cause, but from the slow, grinding toll it took on a man's body.

"I understand the risks," Tom said. "But I need the wages."

Grant studied him. "This have anything to do with your mother being ill?"

"Partly," Tom said, not entirely lying. His mother's health was always a concern, though not the reason for his sudden need for money.

Grant sighed. "I can't stop you. But I won't take you back on the looms when your lungs give out."

"Fair enough." Tom extended his hand. "When can I start?"

"Tonight, if you're that eager to kill yourself." Grant shook Tom's hand briefly. "Report to Michaels at ten. He runs the night crew."

"Thank you, sir."

Tom turned to leave, but Grant called after him. "Hartley."

"Yes, sir?"

"Whatever you're doing this for… make sure it's worth it."

Tom nodded and stepped out of the office into the corridor, the distant thunder of machinery vibrating through the floorboards. As he headed back toward the workshop floor, he saw two figures approaching from the opposite direction, the mill owner, Mr. Harding, and beside him, the slim, well-dressed figure of Silas Drake.

Tom slowed his pace, pretending to check something in his pocket as they passed.

"Profits up fifteen percent since the new machinery, Drake," Harding was saying. "Your investment is already showing returns."

"Excellent," Drake replied, his voice smooth. "And the labor reductions we discussed?"

"Twenty men let go last week. Another fifteen by month's end."

"Good, good. Less wages, more profit."

Their voices faded as they entered Harding's office, but Tom had heard enough. Drake wasn't just lending money to desperate workers, he was investing in the very machinery that put them out of work, creating the conditions that drove them to his door.

The pieces clicked into place. Drake's web was larger than Tom had imagined, stretching from the highest levels of town business down to the poorest workers. A perfect trap, baited with desperation and sprung with calculated precision.

Back on the workshop floor, Tom's hands moved automatically through the familiar motions, but his mind was elsewhere, on Annie Sutherland and her father, on Drake's cold smile, on the fifteen pounds needed to save the cobbler's shop.

The regular shift ended at six. Tom collected his pay and hurried out into the early evening air. He had four hours before his boiler room shift began. Enough time to run his errand.

His first stop was Phillips' Pharmacy on the high street. The bell tinkled as he entered, and Mr. Phillips looked up from behind the counter.

"Tom Hartley, isn't it? Your mother sent you for her tonic?"

"Not today, Mr. Phillips." Tom approached the counter. "I need a bottle of the lung medicine. The one Doctor Perkins prescribes for consumption."

Phillips raised an eyebrow. "Three shillings, that is. And it requires a prescription."

Tom placed the coins on the counter. "It's for Harold Sutherland. The cobbler. Doctor Perkins prescribed it last week."

"Ah, yes." Phillips nodded. "Poor man. Been ill a long while now."

While Phillips prepared the medicine, Tom scribbled a note on a scrap of paper. When he took the wrapped bottle, he hesitated.

"Mr. Phillips, could you tell me... has Miss Sutherland been in for her father's medicine this week?"

Phillips looked uncomfortable. "I shouldn't discuss my customers."

"Of course. I understand." Tom nodded and turned to go.

"She hasn't," Phillips called after him. "And she should have. The bottle I gave her last week would be empty by now."

Tom thanked him and stepped back into the

street. His suspicion confirmed, Annie couldn't afford to refill her father's prescription.

The cobbler's shop was two streets over. Tom approached cautiously, checking that no one was watching. The closed sign hung in the window, but through the glass, he could see a lamp burning in the back workroom. Annie would be there, working by lamplight to save the cost of coal.

Tom crept to the door and placed the package on the step. He tucked his note under the string and knocked firmly before retreating to a shadowed doorway across the street.

A minute passed. Then the door opened, and Annie appeared, looking first left, then right. Her face was tired, her hair coming loose from its pins after a long day. She looked down and saw the package. Confusion crossed her face as she bent to pick it up.

Tom watched as she read his note. Even from across the street, he could see the struggle in her posture. She looked up again, scanning the street, and for a moment, Tom thought she had spotted him. But then she clutched the package to her chest and stepped back inside, closing the door firmly.

His note had been simple: *"Found this among my*

mother's things. She no longer needs it, but thought your father might. —Tom"

A lie, but a necessary one. Annie could accept unused medicine from a neighbor's cupboard more easily than she could accept that Tom had spent his last few shillings to buy it for her father.

Tom waited a moment longer, making sure she didn't come back out to return the package. When the door remained closed, he allowed himself a smile of satisfaction.

With three hours left before his night shift, Tom walked to the small room he rented in a boarding house near the mill. He needed to eat and rest before facing the boiler room.

His landlady, Mrs. Briggs, called out as he passed her kitchen. "Supper's on the table, Mr. Hartley. Stew and bread. Better eat while it's hot."

Tom hadn't planned to spend money on a meal, but the mention of stew made his stomach growl. "Thank you, Mrs. Briggs. I'll be right down."

He washed quickly at the basin in his room, changed his shirt, and joined the other boarders at the long table in the dining room. Besides himself, there were two other mill workers, an old railway man, and a clerk from the post office.

"Heard you've taken the boiler room night shift,

Hartley," said Matthews, one of the mill workers. "Gone soft in the head, have you?"

"Just need the extra wages," Tom replied, breaking off a piece of bread.

"Extra wages won't help when you're dead," Matthews said, shaking his head. "My cousin worked the boilers for six months. He coughed blood for a year after."

"I won't be there that long," Tom assured him. "Just until I save enough."

"Enough for what?" asked Taylor, the postal clerk. "Must be something important to risk the boiler room."

Tom focused on his stew. "My mother's roof needs replacing before winter."

It wasn't entirely a lie. The roof did need work. But Tom didn't mention that his real goal was saving fifteen pounds to pay the Sutherlands' rent.

"Noble son," Matthews said without sarcasm. "But take care of yourself too. No use having a mother with a good roof if her son's in the ground."

At half past nine, he set out for the mill again. The streets were quiet, most families already behind closed doors. As he passed the Fox and Hound, raucous laughter spilled out into the night. For a moment, Tom envied the men inside, drinking away their troubles instead of walking into the mouth of the mill for another shift.

The night entrance to the mill was at the back, near the loading docks. Tom showed his work card to the night watchman, who waved him through with a grunt. "Boiler room's that way. Michaels is expecting you."

The sound of the boilers grew louder as Tom descended the iron stairs to the basement level. Heat rolled up to meet him, along with the smell of coal and hot metal and sweat. By the time he reached the bottom, his shirt was already sticking to his back.

The boiler room stretched the length of the mill, a cavernous space filled with the massive iron furnaces that powered the steam engines. Men moved in the dim light, shoveling coal, checking pressure gauges, adjusting valves. Their faces and clothes were black with coal dust, their movements slow in the crushing heat.

"Hartley?" A bear of a man approached, wiping hands on a rag that might once have been white. "I'm Michaels. Grant said you'd be joining us."

"Yes, sir." Tom extended his hand. "Reporting for work."

Michaels' handshake was firm, his palm callused

from years of handling hot metal. "Ever worked a boiler before?"

"No, sir."

"Didn't think so. You're too pretty." Michaels grinned, revealing teeth startlingly white against his coal-blackened face. "Don't worry. You'll be filthy as the rest of us soon enough."

He led Tom through the room, explaining the work as they went. "Four boilers, each needs feeding every twenty minutes. Coal pile's over there. Fill your barrow, wheel it to the boiler, shovel it in. Simple work, but it'll break your back if you're not careful."

Tom nodded, taking in the oppressive heat, the dim lighting, the men moving like ghosts through the haze of coal dust and steam.

"Shifts are eight hours. No breaks except to piss or get water." Michaels pointed to a barrel in the corner. "Drink plenty. Men who don't end up face-down on the floor."

"Understood."

"You'll work with Davidson tonight. He'll show you the ropes." Michaels gestured to a thin man shoveling coal into one of the boilers. "Questions?"

"No, sir."

"Good. Get to work then."

Davidson looked up as Tom approached. He was older than Tom, perhaps forty, with a permanent stoop to his shoulders and deep lines etched around his eyes.

"You the new man?" he asked, not pausing in his shoveling.

"Tom Hartley."

"Robert Davidson. Grab that other shovel and help me feed this monster."

Tom picked up the shovel and began mimicking Davidson's movements, finding the rhythm of scoop, lift, throw. The heat from the open furnace was like a physical blow, searing his face and hands.

"Keep your head turned when you throw," Davidson advised. "Or your eyebrows'll burn off in a week."

Tom learned the patterns of the boiler room. When to feed the fires, how to check the pressure gauges, when to open the steam valves. The work wasn't complex, but the conditions made every task a struggle. The heat was like nothing Tom had ever experienced. It was like a living thing that pressed against his skin, forced its way into his lungs, sapped his strength with each passing minute.

By midnight, Tom's shirt was soaked through with sweat, his face streaked with coal dust turned to mud by perspiration. His arms ached from shoveling, and each breath pulled hot, dust-filled air into his lungs, making him cough.

"Water break," Davidson said, straightening with a groan. "Come on."

They walked to the water barrel, where Davidson dipped a ladle and handed it to Tom. The water was warm and had a metallic taste, but Tom drank greedily, feeling it run down his parched throat.

"First night's the worst," Davidson said, taking his turn with the ladle. "The body doesn't know what hit it."

"Does it get easier?" Tom asked.

Davidson laughed, a sound like stones rattling in a tin can. "No. You just get used to feeling half-dead."

They returned to their boiler, resuming the endless cycle of feeding the hungry furnace. As they worked, Tom found his mind drifting despite the physical demands of the job.

"Can I ask why you're here?" he said during a brief lull. "Most men avoid the boiler room if they can."

Davidson paused, leaning on his shovel. "Same reason as most. Need the money."

"Family to support?"

"Wife and four children." Davidson wiped sweat

from his brow, leaving a fresh streak of coal dust. "And a debt that never seems to get smaller no matter how much I pay."

Tom thought of Drake and his calculating smile. "Debt to who?"

Davidson gave him a sharp look. "Why do you ask?"

"Just curious."

After a moment's hesitation, Davidson sighed. "Drake. I borrowed ten pounds last year when my youngest was sick. I should've been paid off by now, but somehow the interest keeps growing."

Tom nodded, unsurprised. "How much do you owe now?"

"Fifteen pounds. More than I started with, and that's after making payments every month for a year." Davidson spat on the floor. "Man's a bloodsucker."

"How does he get away with it?"

"He has friends in high places. He owns half the businesses in town through loans and investments." Davidson lowered his voice, though no one could hear them over the roar of the boilers. "And he has ways of making sure people pay."

"What kind of ways?"

"Men who visit your home at night. Accidents at

work." Davidson's face darkened. "Or he offers to let your wife or daughter work off the debt in one of his buildings down by the docks."

Tom felt his hands tighten on the shovel. "That can't be legal."

"Legal?" Davidson laughed bitterly. "Who's to stop him? The magistrate plays cards with him every Thursday. The constable's brother-in-law manages one of Drake's warehouses."

The picture emerging was worse than Tom had imagined. It was a web of corruption and fear that held the town in its grip, with Drake at the center, pulling the strings.

"You're new to night shift," Davidson said, studying Tom. "What brought you here?"

Tom hesitated. "Need money for my mother's roof."

"Roof, is it?" Davidson didn't look convinced. "Most men who end up here are running from something or desperate for something. Which are you?"

"Desperate, I suppose," Tom admitted.

"For what?"

Tom thought of Annie "To help someone who won't accept help."

Understanding dawned in Davidson's eyes. "Ah. A woman."

"Not like that," Tom protested, though the heat in his face wasn't entirely from the boilers. "Just a family that's fallen on hard times."

"Davidson! Hartley! Boiler three needs feeding! Move!"

ANNIE

"Sign here, and here. And initial here. And here."

Drake's clerk pointed to four different places on the loan document, his fingernail yellowed and sharp. Annie hesitated, pen poised above the paper. The terms were written in language that made her head swim, phrases about "compounding interest structures" and "variable repayment schedules" that she pretended to understand.

The five pounds sat on the desk before her. Not enough to clear their debt, but enough to buy time. Enough to keep a roof over their heads for a few more weeks.

Her hand trembled slightly as she signed her

name, Annie Elizabeth Sutherland, on each line. With each stroke of the pen, she felt a weight settle on her shoulders, like the loan was a physical thing climbing onto her back.

"Excellent," the clerk said, taking back the pen and blotting the signatures. "That concludes our business, Miss Sutherland."

He counted out five sovereigns, pushing them across the desk. Five gold coins that would determine her future. Annie placed them carefully in her purse.

"Mr. Drake regrets he could not finalize this transaction personally," the clerk said. "He was called away on other business."

Annie felt only relief at Drake's absence. His cold eyes and smile had haunted her since their meeting two days ago.

"If I might make a suggestion," the clerk continued, folding the loan document. "Should you find the repayment schedule difficult to maintain, Mr. Drake owns the cotton factory on Mill Street. They often need worker. The wage is regular, and arrangements can be made regarding your debt."

Annie stood up, clutching her purse. "I'll manage the payments."

The clerk gave her a smile that didn't reach his eyes. "Of course. But should your circumstances change, remember the offer. Good day, Miss Sutherland."

Outside, the spring sunlight felt harsh after the gloom of Drake's office. Annie stood on the steps, the weight of the coins in her purse both a comfort and a curse. Seven pounds. Less than she needed, but more than she'd had yesterday.

Her first stop was Phillips' Pharmacy. She needed to buy more medicine for her father before the current bottle, the one Tom had mysteriously "found" in his mother's cupboard, ran out. She suspected Tom had purchased it new but couldn't bring herself to refuse the help when her father's health hung in the balance.

The bell tinkled as she entered the shop. Mr. Phillips looked up from his counter and smiled.

"Miss Sutherland. Good morning to you. How's your father today?"

"Better, thank you," Annie replied. "The medicine seems to be helping his cough."

"Good, good. That's the Whitfield Compound for you. Best thing for lung troubles." Mr. Phillips nodded. "I suppose you're here for another bottle?"

"Yes, please."

While Mr. Phillips prepared the medicine, Annie calculated her expenditures. Three shillings for the medicine. Then to the landlord's agent to pay what she could of their debt. That would leave her with just over four pounds, barely enough for a month of basic supplies.

"Here we are." Mr. Phillips wrapped the bottle in paper. "Three shillings, please."

Annie paid with one of Drake's coins, accepting her change with a polite nod. "Thank you, Mr. Phillips."

"Give my regards to your father," he called as she left.

Next, she walked to Mr. Baxter's office on Bridge Street. The younger Baxter had taken over his father's property business six months ago, and in that time, had transformed from the cheerful boy who once bought peppermints at the shop next door to a stern man in a too-tight waistcoat with a ledger where his heart should be.

The office was small but well-appointed, with a polished desk and leather chairs for clients. Peter Baxter looked up as Annie entered, his expression revealing neither pleasure nor displeasure at her arrival.

"Miss Sutherland. Have you come about the rent?"

"Yes, Mr. Baxter." Annie opened her purse. "I have five pounds toward our debt."

Baxter checked his ledger. "Your outstanding balance is fifteen pounds, three shillings, and sixpence."

Annie frowned. " The notice said fifteen exactly."

"The notice was sent a week ago," Baxter explained, tapping his pencil against the ledger. "Interest continues to accrue at thruppennies per day until payment is received in full."

"That's..." Annie did the calculation in her head. "Almost a shilling a week in interest."

"Standard terms, Miss Sutherland. They're outlined in your lease agreement." Baxter held out his hand. "The five pounds, please."

Annie counted out the coins, placing them in Baxter's palm. "When will we receive another notice?"

"That depends." Baxter wrote out a receipt, his handwriting neat and precise. "The rent for next month will be due in three weeks. Six pounds, ten shillings. So, your new total is sixteen pounds, thirteen shillings, and sixpence."

"Six pounds, ten…" Annie stopped. "We've always paid five pounds."

Baxter didn't look up from his writing. "Market adjustments, Miss Sutherland. Rents throughout town have increased."

"By more than ten percent?"

"Property values on High Street have risen considerably." Baxter handed her the receipt. "We could get ten pounds easily for that location from another tenant."

The implication was clear. Annie tucked the receipt into her purse. "We'll pay the new amount."

"Excellent." Baxter smiled for the first time. "Your father is a respected craftsman. It would be a shame to lose your shop."

Annie left the office with her remaining coins feeling much lighter than they should. Four pounds, ten shillings for next month's rent. Plus, Drake's payment, now a burden for future months. The numbers swirled in her mind, refusing to add up to anything but disaster.

Back at the shop, Annie found her father sitting at the workbench, a boot in his hands. He looked up as she entered, his face thin but his eyes brighter than they'd been in weeks.

"There you are girl. Where've you been all morning?"

"Running errands," Annie said, setting down her purse. "Pa, what are you doing down here? You should be resting."

"Been resting too long." Harold held up the boot he was working on. "Orders won't fill themselves."

Annie took off her shawl and hung it by the door. "Is that Mr. Thompson's boot? I was going to finish it this afternoon."

"Already done, except for the polish." Harold smiled. "That medicine is working wonders. I can breathe without feeling like I'm drowning."

Annie felt a pang of guilt at the mention of the medicine, both for accepting Tom's help and for how much it had cost from Drake's loan.

"That's good, Pa, but don't push yourself too hard."

"Pah." Harold waved a hand. "Been taking it easy too long. Shop's suffering for it."

Annie didn't tell him about the rent increase or the loan from Drake. No need to worry him when he was finally improving. Instead, she made tea, and they worked side by side for the first time in months, Harold handling the delicate stitching while

Annie cut new soles from the leather Molly had brought.

The afternoon passed peacefully, with two customers coming in for repairs and one to collect boots Harold had finished months ago. By evening, Annie felt almost hopeful. With her father able to work again, perhaps they could increase their business. Perhaps Drake's loan would be their salvation rather than their doom.

After closing the shop, she helped her father upstairs.

"You should rest now," she said. "Don't want to undo all your progress."

Harold sat in his chair by the fire. "Made more money today than in the past month. Feels good to be useful again."

Annie prepared a simple supper of bread, cheese, and the last of the ham Mrs. Barnes had traded for fixing her husband's work boots. They ate in comfortable silence, the ticking of the clock on the mantel the only sound in the small room.

"Annie," Harold said finally, setting down his plate. "Where did the money come from?"

She looked up, startled. "What money?"

"For the rent and the medicine. Don't think I didn't notice that bottle's brand new." Harold's eyes, so like her own, fixed on her face. "Tell me you didn't go to Drake."

Annie's silence was answer enough.

Harold closed his eyes. "Oh, girl. I told you never to deal with that man."

"What choice did we have, Pa? Another week and we'd be on the street."

"Better the street than in debt to Silas Drake," Harold said, his voice heavy with disappointment. "Your mother and I worked thirty years to build this business. Never took a loan, never owed a man a penny we couldn't pay."

"And now you're sick, and business is failing, and the rent's gone up," Annie said. "I did what I had to do."

"How much?" Harold asked.

"Seven pounds. Enough to pay part of what we owe and keep us in supplies."

"And what does Drake get in return?"

Annie hesitated. "One penny on the shilling per week."

Harold's face paled. "Twenty percent a month? You agreed to that?"

"It's only until we get on our feet again," Annie insisted. "Now that you're better…"

"Girl, don't you understand? Men like Drake

don't lend money expecting to be paid back. They lend money to own people." Harold leaned forward, his voice urgent. "Your grandfather taught me that. It's why we never borrowed, even in the worst times."

"Well, times are worse now," Annie said, standing to clear the plates. "And the loan is signed. We'll make it work."

Harold watched her move about the kitchen, his expression troubled. "What aren't you telling me?"

Annie kept her back to him, washing the dishes in the small basin. "Nothing, Pa."

"Annie Elizabeth Sutherland. You've never been able to lie to me."

She turned, hands dripping water onto her apron. "The rent's gone up. Five pounds, ten shillings, starting next month."

Harold's shoulders slumped. "So that's his game. Squeeze us from both sides."

"What do you mean?"

"Young Baxter was in here last week, talking with Drake. I heard them from the back room. Didn't think much of it at the time." Harold shook his head. "Drake's buying up properties all over town. Wouldn't surprise me if he's bought our building too."

A cold feeling settled in Annie's stomach. "You think Mr. Baxter sold to Drake?"

"Or Drake's lending him money. Either way, the result's the same." Harold sighed. "We're in a trap, girl. And it's my fault for getting sick."

"It's not your fault," Annie said fiercely. "And we're not trapped. We'll find a way."

But even as she spoke, she wasn't sure she believed it.

That night, after her father went to bed, Annie returned to the shop. A special order waited on her workbench, a pair of dancing shoes for the mayor's daughter, delicate things with thin soles and satin uppers. Annie had promised them for Monday, and they still needed the final stitching and decorative beadwork.

She worked by lamplight, her needle flashing in and out of the soft fabric. The work was precise, requiring all her concentration.

Without realizing it, she began humming an old tune, something her mother used to sing while she worked. The memory of her mother's hands, guiding Annie's small fingers through the first simple stitches, came back with sudden clarity.

"Like this, Annie-girl," her mother had said, voice soft with patience. "Let the needle find its own path. The leather knows where it wants to be joined."

Annie had been six, maybe seven, her legs swinging from the high stool by her mother's workbench. She remembered the smell of leather and polish, the warmth of the shop on a winter afternoon, the contentment of working beside her mother.

That memory led to another, her mother laid in bed, face flushed with fever, hand hot as fire when Annie held it.

"Take care of your father," she'd whispered. "He forgets himself when he works."

"I will, Ma," Annie had promised, not understanding what was happening. Not knowing that by morning, her mother would be gone, leaving Annie and her father to navigate life without her presence.

The shop bell jingled, startling Annie from her memories. She looked up, disoriented, to find morning sunlight streaming through the windows. She'd fallen asleep at her workbench, needle still in hand.

The bell jingled again. It was Sunday. Church would be starting soon. Annie scrambled up, smoothing her rumpled dress and hastily pinning her hair.

"Coming!" she called, hurrying to the door.

Her father stood on the step, fully dressed in his Sunday best, an old suit he kept for church and funerals, brushed and pressed as neatly as Annie could manage with their meager resources.

"Thought you were still abed," Harold said, looking her up and down. "You sleep down here?"

"I fell asleep working on Miss Bax's dancing shoes." Annie held the door for him. "Give me five minutes to change."

"Take ten. Bell hasn't rung yet."

Annie rushed upstairs to wash her face and change into her Sunday dress, a dark blue one that had been her mother's, taken in at the waist and let out at the hem to fit Annie's taller frame. It was old-fashioned and worn thin at the elbows, but clean and respectable. Good enough for church, where half the congregation wore clothes handed down through generations.

When she came back downstairs, her father was waiting patiently, hat in hand. He looked better than he had in weeks, though still too thin, still too pale.

"Ready?" he asked.

"Ready." Annie took his arm, feeling the bones beneath his sleeve. "We can stay home if you're tired."

"Nonsense. Missed too many Sundays already. People will think I've turned heathen."

They walked slowly down High Street toward St. Mark's. The morning was clear and mild, perfect spring weather that brought townspeople out in their Sunday clothes, nodding greetings as they passed.

The church bells began to ring as they approached, calling the faithful to worship. Annie helped her father up the steps, conscious of the eyes watching them, some with sympathy. In a small town, everyone's business was common knowledge, and their struggles would be no secret.

Inside, the church was cool and dim, light filtering through stained glass to cast colorful patterns on the wooden pews. Annie guided her father to their usual seat halfway down the aisle, helping him settle before taking her place beside him.

As the congregation filled in around them, Annie glanced across the aisle. Tom Hartley sat with his mother, a small woman with gray hair and the same kind eyes as her son. Tom was wearing a clean shirt with the collar buttoned tight, and his hair combed back from his forehead. He looked tired, and the shadows under his eyes suggesting he hadn't slept well.

As if feeling her gaze, Tom turned. Their eyes met for a brief moment before Annie looked away, focusing on the hymnal in her hands. But throughout the service, she felt his presence across the aisle, a warmth in the cool church.

Reverend Clarke's sermon was about community and sharing burdens. "No man is an island," he quoted, "We are all connected in God's great plan. The trials of one are the trials of all, and the joys of one, the joys of all."

Annie wondered if the sermon was directed at her, if Reverend Clarke remembered her visit to the poor box. Her father listened intently, nodding at points that resonated with him. Once or twice, Annie's eyes strayed back to Tom, only to find him already looking at her. Each time, they both quickly looked away.

After the final hymn, the congregation filed out, stopping to greet Reverend Clarke at the door. Harold moved slowly, leaning on Annie's arm, but insisted on standing straight when they reached the Reverend.

"Good to see you back with us, Mr. Sutherland,"

Reverend Clarke said, clasping Harold's hand. "You're looking better."

"Feeling better, thank the Lord," Harold replied. "And good medicine."

"Indeed. Both have their place in healing." Reverend Clarke smiled at Annie. "Your father is blessed to have such a devoted daughter."

Annie felt her face warm at the praise. "Thank you, Reverend."

They moved on, making their way down the church steps. The sun was higher now, warming the spring air. People gathered in small groups, exchanging news and pleasantries before heading home to dinner.

"Harold Sutherland! Is that you outside in daylight?"

A booming voice made them turn. Mr. Fletcher, the butcher, approached with his wife on his arm. A large man with a red face and hands like hams, Fletcher had been friends with Harold for years.

"John Fletcher," Harold nodded. "Margaret. Good to see you both."

"And you!" Fletcher clapped Harold on the shoulder, nearly knocking him off balance. "Thought we'd lost you to that cough. How are you feeling?"

"Better every day," Harold assured him. "Soon be back in the shop full time."

"Good, good! I need those new boots I ordered. My winter pair are falling apart." Fletcher turned to Annie. "This girl of yours been keeping the place running, has she?"

"I couldn't manage without her," Harold said, patting Annie's hand on his arm.

Mrs. Fletcher, a thin woman with sharp eyes, looked Annie up and down. "You're too pale, child. Working too hard, I'll wager. You should come to dinner some Sunday. Our Peter asks after you regular."

Annie forced a smile. Peter Fletcher was the butcher's son, a dull-witted boy of nineteen who stared at Annie whenever she entered his father's shop. "Thank you, Mrs. Fletcher. Perhaps when Pa is fully recovered."

The Fletchers moved on, replaced by others wanting to welcome Harold back to church. By the time they'd spoken to everyone, Harold was swaying slightly on his feet, his strength fading.

"We should get you home," Annie said quietly. "You've done enough for one day."

Harold nodded, too tired to argue. They were

halfway down the path when a familiar voice called from behind.

"Mr. Sutherland! Miss Sutherland!"

Tom Hartley approached, his mother beside him. Up close, Annie could see the exhaustion in his face more clearly, the redness around his eyes, the tightness at the corners of his mouth. But he smiled warmly, as if genuinely pleased to see them.

"Good morning," Tom said. "It's good to see you at church, sir. You're looking well."

"Getting there, lad, getting there." Harold shook Tom's hand. "That medicine you found worked wonders."

"Glad to hear it." Tom turned to his mother. "Ma, this is Mr. Sutherland and his daughter, Annie. This is my mother, Sarah Hartley."

"Pleased to meet you both," Sarah said, her voice soft but clear. "I've heard much about your shop. Tom tells me Annie's work is as fine as yours, Mr. Sutherland."

Harold beamed with pride. "Better, some days. Girl has magic in her hands, like her mother did."

Annie felt her face grow warm again. "Pa exaggerates."

"I doubt that" Sarah said kindly. "A good cobbler's skill shows in every step their customers take."

As they spoke, Annie noticed Tom's hands were raw, red skin across the knuckles, a fresh burn on the back of his right hand. The marks of hard, dangerous work. When he saw her looking, Tom tucked his hands behind his back, as if embarrassed by their condition.

"We should let you get home," Sarah said, noticing Harold's fatigue. "The sun's getting high, and it's a warm day for spring."

"May we escort you?" Tom offered. "It's on our way."

Harold started to refuse, but Annie spoke first. "That would be kind, thank you."

She saw surprise flicker across Tom's face before it settled back into a pleasant smile. They fell into step together, Annie and her father in the middle, Tom and his mother on either side. The pace was slow to accommodate both Harold and Sarah, whose limp became more pronounced as they walked.

"Rheumatism," Sarah explained when she caught Annie looking. "Acts up in damp weather."

"My wife suffered the same," Harold said. "Found wrapping the joints in flannel soaked with witch hazel helped some."

"I'll try that, thank you."

They continued the conversation, Harold and

Sarah exchanging remedies for various ailments while Annie and Tom walked in silence. Occasionally their eyes would meet, and Annie would look quickly away, unsure why her heart seemed to beat faster when he was near.

As they reached the cobbler shop, Harold turned to Tom. "Thank you for the escort, young man. And for the medicine. Good of you to think of us."

"Just being neighborly, sir." Tom's gaze flickered to Annie. "My mother always says a community must look after its own."

Harold fumbled with his key. "You and Mrs. Hartley must come for tea sometime."

"We'd be honored," Sarah said before Tom could respond. "Perhaps next Sunday?"

"Excellent!" Harold beamed, his earlier fatigue seemingly forgotten in the pleasure of socializing. "After church, then."

Annie watched this exchange with a mixture of alarm and resignation. Her father's loneliness had been as much a burden as his illness. How could she refuse him this small pleasure, even if it meant enduring Tom's company?

"Well, good day to you both," Harold said, finally getting the door open. "Until next Sunday."

"Good day, Mr. Sutherland. Miss Sutherland."

Tom tipped his hat, his eyes lingering on Annie's face.

As he turned to leave, the sleeve of his coat rode up, revealing another raw and angry burn on his wrist. Annie spoke without thinking.

"Mr. Hartley, your hand. You're hurt."

Tom quickly pulled his sleeve down. "It's nothing. Just a small accident at the mill."

"Mill work isn't known for 'small' accidents," Harold said, frowning. "What happened, boy?"

"Boiler room," Tom admitted. "I took an extra shift, and my hand slipped on a hot valve."

"Boiler room?" Harold's frown deepened. "Dangerous place. Men die there regular from the heat and the coal dust."

"It's just temporary," Tom assured him. "For the extra wages, you know."

Annie stared at the covered burn, remembering what Molly had told her about men taking dangerous work to pay off Drake's loans. "You shouldn't risk your health for money," she said, the words coming out harsher than she intended.

Tom's expression closed. "Sometimes risks are necessary, Miss Sutherland."

An uncomfortable silence fell between them.

Sarah patted her son's arm. "We should continue home, Tom. I need to rest before dinner."

"Of course, Ma." Tom nodded to Annie and her father. "Good day to you both."

As they walked away, Annie caught Sarah glancing back with a knowing look that made Annie's face warm again. She hurried her father inside, closing the door firmly behind them.

"Nice young man," Harold said as Annie helped him to his chair. "Works hard, takes care of his mother. Reminds me of myself at that age."

"He's just being neighborly," Annie said, echoing Tom's words. "No need to make more of it."

"Didn't say a word about 'more,' did I?" Harold's eyes twinkled with mischief. "Though he certainly looks at you like I used to look at your mother."

"Pa!" Annie busied herself putting the kettle on for tea. "Don't talk nonsense."

"Not nonsense, girl. I have eyes in my head." Harold chuckled. "And I saw those burns on his hands too. Boiler room work pays extra for a reason. Boy's working himself to death for something."

"Or someone," Annie muttered, remembering the medicine, the doctor's fee, and Tom's persistent offers of help.

"What's that?"

"Nothing, Pa." Annie set cups on the table. "Just thinking the Hartley's seem like good people."

"That they do." Harold nodded. "That they do."

As Annie prepared their Sunday tea, her mind returned to the image of Tom's burned hands, to the exhaustion in his face, to the way his eyes had sought hers during church. Something was happening that she didn't fully understand, but it felt like a door opening, just a crack, letting in a sliver of light where before there had been only shadow.

TOM

"You don't see the way he looked at me, Tom? Like I was dirt under his boot."

Tom wiped sweat from his neck with the back of his hand. The mill floor was loud, the looms clattering without pause. He and Billy stood by the open loading dock, gulping air that was only slightly cleaner than inside.

"What did he say?" Tom asked.

Billy's hands were balled into fists. "Said my pa had until Friday. No extensions. No more excuses. If we can't pay, he'll take something else."

Tom felt a familiar anger rise. "Drake's men?"

Billy nodded, his jaw tight. "Two of them. One was the usual, skinny fellow with bad teeth. The other..." He shivered, like the memory itself made his skin crawl. "Was bigger. A big scar on his cheek and I never seen him before."

Tom had. The scarred man worked the docks on occasion, handling crates with hands the size of hammers. He had a reputation. Fights in alleys, debts that never got settled the fair way.

"What did your pa say?"

Billy let out a slow breath. "Nothing he could say. They weren't asking. Just warning."

Tom glanced around the yard. The lunch whistle had blown, and men gathered in their usual spots. Most ate in silence, heads down. Others whispered in clusters, their voices had the same tension as Billy's.

He caught snatches of conversations.

"Drake sent a man to my door last night…"

"Said they'd dock my pay directly if I don't settle by week's end…"

"Lost my overtime shift, and now he wants full payment by Monday? How am I supposed to…"

Tom exhaled slowly. He had seen the pattern before, but today, it was clearer. Drake was moving in. First, he would offer small loans to workers barely making enough to survive. Then, pressure them. A few men, a few threats, all at once. Keep everyone scared, keep them isolated. Make sure they knew no one was coming to save them.

Billy kicked at a loose stone. "Pa ain't got the money, Tom. We barely eat as it is. What's he gonna do?"

Tom didn't have an answer.

A whistle blew, signaling the end of lunch. The men groaned, some still chewing as they stood. Billy gave Tom a look, half defiance, half fear, before heading back inside.

Tom followed, his mind working as hard as his hands through the next few hours.

By the time his shift ended, his shoulders burned, and his legs felt like lead. He had barely slept in days, running on whatever stale bread and cold meat he could afford between shifts. He had to be careful. Exhaustion made a man sloppy, and in the boiler room, that meant worse than lost wages.

He pulled his boots on tighter, rubbing his heel where the sole had begun to thin. That gave him an idea.

Tom left the mill, cutting through the narrow streets until he reached Sutherland's Cobbler Shop. The bell above the door jingled as he stepped inside.

Annie looked up from behind the counter. This

time, she didn't immediately frown at the sight of him.

"Mr. Hartley."

"Miss Sutherland."

He set a pair of boots on the counter. "I got another repair for you."

Annie wiped her hands on her apron before picking up one of the boots. "Yours?"

"A friend's," Tom said, which wasn't entirely a lie. "Needs them patched up proper."

She turned the boot over, inspecting the heel, the stitching. "Factory make."

Tom gave a slight shrug. "Most boots are these days."

Annie clicked her tongue but didn't argue. "These need more than just patching. The heel's splitting. Whoever owns these must walk heavy on one side."

"That a problem?"

"No. Just means the repair won't hold unless I reset the balance."

Tom nodded. He watched as she moved, reaching for tools, testing the leather between her fingers. She was focused, efficient. A master of her craft.

He leaned against the counter, eyes drifting to a paper tucked near the till. The ink was still fresh.

Half PAID

Next to it sat neatly stacked leather, new and untouched.

Tom didn't ask. He didn't have to.

"Two shillings now," Annie said, setting the boots aside, "the rest when they're done."

Tom counted the coins onto the counter.

Annie hesitated, then reached for the kettle on the small stove. "Tea?"

Tom almost laughed at the unexpected offer but caught himself. "If you've got enough."

She poured two cups, pushing one toward him.

"Your hands are shaking," she said, looking at his fingers curled around the cup.

Tom glanced down. She wasn't wrong. The long shifts, the heat, the lack of sleep was catching up.

"I am just tired," he said.

Annie didn't press. They drank in silence, the warmth of the tea cutting through the stiffness of the moment.

"You've been working nights," she said finally.

Tom looked at her over the rim of his cup. "Word travels."

"Word travels when a man suddenly takes on double shifts in the worst part of the mill."

Tom set his cup down. "It pays better."

"And costs more," Annie said. She nodded toward his hands. "The burns, blisters. I've seen it before."

"Man's got to do what he must," Tom said.

Annie gave a small nod. "So he does."

The bell above the door jingled. A customer entered, and Annie's attention shifted. Tom finished his tea and stood.

"Friday, then," he said, tapping the counter near the boots.

"Friday," Annie confirmed.

Tom stepped outside. The night air was thick, damp with the promise of rain. He pulled his collar up and made his way toward the mill.

The boiler room was worse than usual.

Heat pressed in from all sides, thick and suffocating. The machines roared, steam hissing from the pipes. The coal dust clung to everything.

Tom shoveled, sweat running down his back. The hours stretched, his body moving by instinct alone. He could barely see, barely think.

Then it happened.

A slight misstep. A moment's distraction.

The edge of the furnace door caught his arm.

Pain shot through him. The skin burned, raw and stinging. He stumbled back, gritting his teeth.

Davidson, the older worker beside him, grabbed his arm. "You all right, boy?"

Tom nodded, forcing himself to stay steady.

"Go see the mill doctor," Davidson said. "Don't need you dropping dead down here."

Tom didn't argue. He left the shovel and climbed the steps toward the mill infirmary.

The doctor, a thin, balding man with wire-rimmed glasses, barely looked up as Tom entered. "Another one?"

Tom sat, rolling up his sleeve. The burn was red, angry looking. The doctor hummed, dabbing something foul-smelling onto the wound.

"Seen three men this week alone with burns like this," the doctor muttered.

"Accidents happen," Tom said.

The doctor shook his head. "Not this often. Not before Drake started throwing money at the mill."

Tom frowned. "What does that have to do with anything?"

The doctor wrapped the wound. "Machines break down. Parts need replacing. Takes money to do that. So, what happens when a man like Drake lends the mill owner funds?"

Tom exhaled. "The money doesn't go to the machines."

The doctor nodded. "It goes where profit is made fastest. Hiring more men to work longer, pushing the ones already here past their limits. But maintenance? Safety? Not as profitable."

Tom flexed his fingers. The bandage pulled against his skin.

Drake's reach was deeper than he had thought.

It wasn't just the workers trapped in his debt. The whole town was caught in his hands.

Tom stood. "Thanks, Doc."

The doctor nodded. "Try not to get burned again."

Tom left the infirmary, heading back into the night. His arm throbbed, his head pounded.

He needed to sleep.

But he knew he wouldn't.

Not now.

Not with everything starting to make sense.

ANNIE

"That can't be right."

Annie held the receipt in both hands, staring at the inked numbers. The clerk, a thin man with sharp eyes, sat behind the high counter, tapping his fingers against the polished wood.

"It's correct, Miss Sutherland," he said without looking at her. "One pound, five shillings is the required payment for this month."

"But I gave you one pound, five shillings," she said, pressing the receipt flat. "That should bring my balance down."

The clerk sighed, as if explaining to a child. "That covers the interest."

Annie felt something cold settle in her chest. "The interest?"

"Yes," the clerk said, still not meeting her eyes. "Your principal remains unchanged."

Annie swallowed. "That's not what he told me. Mr. Drake said…"

The clerk slid a paper across the counter. "The contract, Miss Sutherland."

She stared at the familiar sheet, her own signature at the bottom. The words swam before her eyes, the same careful script she had read when Drake first placed it in front of her. But now, the clerk pointed to a section near the bottom, where the ink was smaller, the sentences pressed tightly together.

"Interest charged at one shilling per pound per month. Payment of interest required before any principal deduction may occur."

Annie gripped the edge of the counter. "I don't understand."

The clerk finally looked up, "Each month, you must pay the interest first. Only after that can any additional payment be applied to what you owe. If you continue to pay one pound, five shillings, you will remain in debt indefinitely."

Annie's breath caught. "That's not what he said. Mr. Drake told me…"

"Mr. Drake explained the terms fairly," the clerk

said, "You signed the contract, Miss Sutherland. The terms are binding."

Annie shook her head. "But if I pay the full amount in a few months…"

The clerk placed a finger on another section of the paper. "*Failure to repay the full amount within the agreed period will result in an automatic increase in the interest rate, as determined by the lender.*"

She stared at the words.

"I borrowed seven pounds," she whispered.

"And you still owe seven pounds," the clerk confirmed. "Unless, of course, you would like to increase your payments. Then we can begin discussing the reduction of your balance."

Annie felt dizzy. The shop had been quiet all week. Repairs barely covered food and coal. The rent would be due again soon.

"How much do I need to pay to start reducing what I owe?" she asked.

The clerk looked back at the ledger. "Two pounds, ten shillings this month. Then next month, slightly less, assuming no penalties occur."

Annie blinked. "Penalties?"

"The contract states," the clerk continued, flipping to another page, "that any late payment results in an additional charge. Failure to meet the required minimum will increase your interest rate. There are also fees for processing and collection, should our agents need to visit your premises."

Annie's stomach turned. "What kind of fees?"

"That depends on the situation," the clerk said, adjusting his cuffs. "If payment is simply late, the penalty is three shillings. If a visit is required, five shillings. If legal action must be considered, additional costs apply."

Annie pressed her palm against her forehead.

The money she had given today was everything she had managed to save, and it had done nothing. She could scrape together another one pound, five shillings next month, and the month after, and she would still owe the same.

She could never pay it back.

"Miss Sutherland," the clerk said, in a tone that was almost polite. "This is why it is best to read before signing."

Annie clenched her jaw. "I did read it."

"Then you understood the terms."

"I…" She stopped. She had read it. But not carefully enough. The words had seemed fair, the numbers reasonable. But she hadn't known about this.

Drake had not mentioned this.

The clerk folded the contract again. "I would advise you to make your next payment on time. It prevents… complications."

Annie slid her hands off the counter, curling them into fists.

"Good day, Miss Sutherland," the clerk said, nodding toward the door.

She turned, moving through the office in a daze. The heavy door swung open, letting in cold air. She stepped outside, feeling the street under her boots but not truly aware of it.

The buildings stretched around her, the hum of the market drifting from further down. Horses clattered past with carts full of goods.

She barely saw any of it.

Her debt had not changed. She had been tricked.

A voice rose behind her.

"Miss Sutherland!"

Annie turned.

It was Drake. He stood on the steps of the bank, fastening his gloves. His coat was fine, his hat sharp. He looked as if the cold did not touch him at all.

He smiled, as if they were old friends. "I trust your visit went well."

Annie stared at him.

"You made your first payment," he continued,

stepping down onto the street. "A fine thing, to settle one's debts. It shows character."

Her fingers curled tighter. "You lied to me."

Drake's brows lifted. "I did no such thing."

"You said…" Her throat felt tight. "You said I could pay it back in time. That the terms were fair."

"And they are," Drake said, as if explaining the weather. "I told you the rate. I told you the amount. I told you the terms were standard."

"You did not tell me the payments only covered interest."

Drake tilted his head. "Did I not?"

Annie's jaw locked.

He smiled. "Miss Sutherland, you are a businesswoman. Surely you understand the importance of agreements. I presented you with terms. You accepted them. That is how business is done."

She wanted to scream. "I will repay the loan."

"Of course you will."

"In full."

His smile widened. "I look forward to it."

Annie turned on her heel and walked. She did not wait for another word.

The market was crowded when she arrived. But all she could see was the receipt in her hand, the numbers glaring at her.

"Annie?"

She blinked. Molly stood in front of her, a basket on her arm, a frown on her face.

"You alright?"

Annie nodded, folding the receipt and tucking it into her pocket. "Fine."

"You look like you're ready to strangle someone."

Annie inhaled, glancing at the stalls around them.

Molly tilted her head. "This about the shop?"

Annie hesitated. She could say yes. She could say she was just worried about orders or the cost of leather. But the words felt heavy in her throat.

Before she could speak, another voice broke in.

"If it's money trouble, you won't find answers here."

Annie turned.

A woman stood next to Molly. Her coat was worn, and the sleeves patched at the elbows. She held herself straight, but Annie saw the stiffness in her posture, the way her fingers twitched at her sides.

"This is Marie," Molly said, shifting the basket on her arm. "She worked at Drake's factory."

Marie let out a breath. "Worked. Not anymore."

Annie's hands tightened at her sides.

"Fired?"

Marie let out a dry sound that wasn't quite a laugh. "You could call it that. They threw me out soon as I couldn't keep up."

Molly's mouth pressed into a thin line. "She got hurt."

Annie looked at Marie's arm. The sleeve hung loose, but the shape of it was wrong.

Marie caught her glance and lifted the fabric. A thick bandage covered her wrist, wrapping up to her forearm.

"Caught in the gears," she said. "A second slower, and I'd have lost the whole hand."

Annie's stomach turned.

"Doctor at the factory said it wasn't too bad," Marie continued, lowering her arm. "Wrapped it up, sent me back to work the next day."

Annie frowned. "You went back?"

Marie's eyes darkened. "Didn't have a choice. If you miss a shift, they take it from your pay. So, I went back. Tried to work, but I couldn't keep pace." She flexed her fingers. "By the third day, they docked my wages for 'slowing the line.' By the fifth, they let me go."

Molly exhaled through her nose. "She was in debt before they even threw her out."

Annie felt her pulse quicken. "They made you pay for getting hurt?"

Marie gave her a look. "You think Drake runs that place to lose money?"

Annie's throat felt tight. "I thought…" She shook her head. She hadn't thought.

Marie rubbed the back of her neck. "It's all a trick. Wages seem decent, but then they fine you for everything. Come in a minute late? Half a day's pay gone. Speak out of turn? A shilling gone. Touch the machine wrong? Another." She shook her head. "And the worst part? The fines don't go to the factory. They go straight back to Drake."

Molly crossed her arms. "She's not the only one. I know three others who were let go in the last month, all with debt they can't pay."

Marie's jaw tightened. "The work's fast, the air's thick, the machines don't stop. You make a mistake, you pay. If you can't pay, they take your job. Then what do you do? You owe money, but now you've got nothing to earn it back."

Annie felt her hands shake. This was the same trick Drake had played on her.

"You owe him forever," she whispered.

Marie's gaze met hers. "That's the point."

A cart rattled past, hooves clattering on the stone road. Annie barely noticed.

Marie crossed her arms. "I heard about you, you know. Word gets around. You borrowed from him, didn't you?"

Annie didn't answer.

Marie nodded, as if she already knew. "Then take it from me. You won't ever finish paying it back. Not how he wants."

Annie exhaled. "Then how do I get free?"

Marie's mouth twisted. "You don't."

TOM

Tom shifted the sack of coal higher onto his shoulder and his body protested the effort, sore from the long hours at the mill, but he kept moving. The cold was biting today, and the sooner he finished his deliveries, the sooner people would have warmth in their homes.

The church's charity committee sent out coal to those who needed it most, the elderly, the widowed, the families scraping by. Tom had volunteered years ago, back when he could spare the time. Now, between shifts at the mill and the boiler room, it was harder, but he still showed up when he could.

He climbed the steps to Mrs. Winters' cottage, balancing the sack against his hip as he knocked.

The door creaked open, and a familiar, wrinkled face peered out.

"Ah, Tom, bless you," Mrs. Winters said, pulling her shawl tighter around her thin frame. "Come in, lad, before the cold takes you too."

He stepped inside, careful not to drop coal dust onto the worn rug. The small sitting room smelled of damp wood and lavender, the fire in the hearth barely flickering.

"Where do you want it?" he asked.

"Back by the stove, dear," she said, nodding toward the kitchen.

Tom carried the sack through the narrow doorway and lowered it gently near the iron stove. His shoulders ached as he straightened. The warmth of the kitchen was weak, the coals from yesterday already burned low.

"You need more kindling," he said.

Mrs. Winters sighed. "Aye, I know. Been trying to make do."

Tom wiped his hands on his trousers. "I can bring some by tomorrow."

"You're a good boy, Tom," she said, "Your mother raised you right."

He was about to respond when another voice drifted from the sitting room.

"Ma, we don't have a choice."

Tom paused.

"I know you want to hold on to them, but if we don't pay, they'll come to collect. You know what that means."

He stepped quietly back toward the doorway, stopping just before the threshold.

Mrs. Winters' daughter, Margaret, stood near the hearth, her arms crossed, her face drawn with worry.

Her mother shook her head. "Those rings were your grandmother's."

"I know," Margaret said, her voice tight. "But they won't take sentiment as payment. I went to see Mr. Drake's clerk yesterday. We owe more than I thought."

Tom felt his chest tighten.

Mrs. Winters sat down heavily in her chair. "How much?"

"More than we can manage." Margaret's fingers twisted together. "And that's just this month. If we don't find the rest, they'll add another fee. It never stops."

Mrs. Winters covered her mouth with her hand. "We'll find a way."

Margaret let out a slow breath. "We have to sell

them, Ma. It's better than what happens if we don't."

He cleared his throat, stepping back into the room. Margaret startled, pressing a hand to her chest.

"Tom," she said, forcing a smile. "Didn't hear you come in."

"Didn't mean to eavesdrop," he said.

Mrs. Winters smoothed her hands over her skirt, her expression guarded now. "We're grateful for the coal, dear."

Tom nodded. If they had another option, they would take it. But they didn't. Neither did half the families in this district.

Tom picked up his cap. "I'll be back with the kindling tomorrow."

Margaret nodded. "Thank you, Tom."

Tom returned to the factory and the looms clattered, the air thick with cotton dust. Tom guided the shuttle with one hand, his movements sharp and precise. His body ached from the morning's work, but there was no time for weariness. At the mill, a man who slowed down was a man who didn't last.

A murmur rippled through the workshop floor. Heads turned toward the upper walkway, where Mr. Harding, the mill owner, walked alongside a familiar figure.

Tom didn't have to guess who it was.

Silas Drake moved with ease, his coat unbuttoned, his posture relaxed. His boots were polished, his gloves crisp. He wasn't a man who had ever dirtied his hands in a place like this.

Tom watched as Harding gestured toward the machinery, speaking in a tone just loud enough for those below to hear.

"Profits are strong this quarter," Harding said. "The investment you made into the expansion has already begun paying off."

Drake smiled. "Good to hear."

Harding led him further along the walkway, pointing to the new looms in the far section. "With these, production increases, but labor costs remain the same."

Drake's gaze flicked down toward the workers, watching them without expression.

Tom clenched his jaw.

"Next year," Harding continued, "we expect to cut another ten percent of staff while doubling our output."

Drake nodded. "Efficiency is key, Mr. Harding. The faster you control overhead, the more profitable you remain."

Tom tightened his grip on the shuttle, feeling the rough edge of the wood press against his palm.

They weren't talking about machines. They were talking about people.

Drake clasped his hands behind his back. "And the properties?"

Harding hesitated. "I've sent the inquiries. Some owners are reluctant to sell."

Drake let out a low chuckle. "They won't be for long. Keep pressing. If necessary, I have associates who can apply…persuasion."

Tom exhaled through his nose, forcing himself to focus on his work.

The two men continued past, their conversation fading into the hum of machinery.

Jack, the older mill worker, leaned toward Tom as soon as they were out of earshot.

"Did you hear that?"

Tom gave a short nod.

Jack wiped his forehead with his sleeve. "They're buying everything they can get their hands on."

Tom turned his head slightly. "What do you mean?"

Jack kept his eyes on his loom, but his voice dropped. "Word around town is Drake's got men buying up shops, houses, even the old tannery lot. But they ain't buying in his name."

Tom frowned. "Who, then?"

"Proxy buyers," Jack said. "Men with clean records, people no one would suspect. By the time anyone realizes who owns what, it's too late."

If he owned the working district, the businesses, and the rental homes, he owned the people inside them.

He could set the rents. He could decide who stayed and who left.

Tom ran a hand through his hair. "And nobody's stopping him?"

Jack let out a short, bitter laugh. "Who's going to? The magistrate rents his office from one of Drake's men. The constable's cousin works for him. Even the mayor…" Jack shook his head. "The ones with power don't want to fight him. The rest of us can't."

Drake's web stretched further than he had imagined.

And from all indication, he wasn't finished yet.

ANNIE

The bell above the shop door chimed. Annie looked up from her work, brushing wood shavings from her apron. Customers had been rare lately. Most repairs had slowed, and new orders had nearly vanished.

A woman stepped inside, her coat fastened neatly at the waist, a silk scarf draped over her shoulders. Annie recognized her at once. She was Mrs. Nazari, wife of the bank manager.

Annie straightened. "Good afternoon, Mrs. Nazari."

The woman offered a polite smile, taking in the shop with a glance. "Miss Sutherland. I hope I'm not interrupting."

"Not at all," Annie said. "How can I help you?"

Mrs. Nazari stepped forward, removing her gloves carefully. "I need a special order. A pair of boots for my husband's birthday. He prefers fine leather, something durable but comfortable. He walks to the bank most mornings, so they must withstand wear."

Annie nodded, reaching for her measuring tape. "I can craft something that suits his needs. How may I take his measurements, or do you have an older pair I can reference?"

Mrs. Nazari lifted a small cloth bundle from her handbag and unfolded it, revealing a well-worn boot. "These are his favorites. He says nothing else fits quite as well."

Annie took the boot, running her fingers along the stitching. The leather had softened over time, molding to the shape of the wearer's foot. She pressed gently along the sole, noting where it had worn thin. "I see the problem. The construction is good, but the support has weakened. I can craft a similar pair, reinforced in the right places."

"That would be excellent," Mrs. Nazari said. She glanced at the shelves behind Annie, where pieces of cut leather waited to be shaped. "It's been some time since I saw handmade work. Fewer artisans these days, it seems."

Annie measured the boot carefully, marking the dimensions on a scrap of paper. "Machines are replacing hands," she said.

Mrs. Nazari sighed. "It's true. Everything is moving toward industry. Even at the bank, we see it. New investors, new business ventures, many of them controlled by a few powerful men."

Annie kept her expression neutral. "You mean Mr. Drake."

Mrs. Nazari's mouth pressed into a thin line. "His name comes up often."

Annie adjusted the measuring tape, folding it neatly. "You deal with him?"

Mrs. Nazari hesitated, as if considering whether to continue. Finally, she lowered her voice. "Not directly. My husband does. He says Drake is expanding, buying up property, taking over businesses. It isn't just loans anymore."

Annie set the boot down. "What else?"

Mrs. Nazari studied her. "Why the interest?"

Annie met her gaze. "A businesswoman should know the landscape she works in."

Mrs. Nazari nodded slowly. "Then you should know this, Mr. Drake doesn't operate alone. He has men in many places. Some in law, some in trade. When he moves, it's because he already has agreements in place. By the time anyone notices, he's already won."

Annie absorbed the words. "And the bank?"

"My husband has concerns," Mrs. Nazari admitted. "Drake doesn't borrow like others. He invests, he buys, he secures land. But not under his name. Always through intermediaries. It makes it difficult to track."

"Has he bought the bank?" Annie asked.

Mrs. Nazari gave a small laugh. "No. Not yet. But he has influence. He knows which accounts struggle, which businesses are failing. He offers help before they ask for it. And once they take it…" She shook her head. "They don't escape."

Annie's fingers curled slightly against the counter.

Mrs. Nazari adjusted her scarf. "Miss Sutherland, if you ever find yourself needing financial assistance, tread carefully. A favor from the wrong man is a debt that never disappears."

Annie forced a polite smile. "I appreciate the warning."

Mrs. Nazari handed her a folded note. "For the deposit."

Annie took it, nodding. "Your order will be ready in two weeks."

Mrs. Nazari smiled, slipping her gloves back on. "I'll return then."

She turned toward the door. "Good day, Miss Sutherland."

"Good day, Mrs. Nazari."

Annie tightened her shawl as she stepped out of the shop, the street was busier now that it was an hour ago.

She didn't know why, but her feet carried her toward Molly's shop.

It wasn't planned. She wasn't even sure what she meant to say when she got there. But something about sitting alone in the shop, trapped with her thoughts, didn't feel right.

The bell above the door jingled as she stepped inside.

Molly was near the back, a pin clenched between her lips, adjusting the hem of a coat on a dress form. She glanced up and grinned when she saw Annie.

"Look at this!" Molly plucked the pin from her mouth. "Miss Sutherland, in my shop! And what's this in your hands? A gift?"

Annie rolled her eyes and held out the folded shirt. "A repair."

Molly took it, shaking it out. "Your father's?"

Annie nodded.

Molly gave a mock frown. "And you didn't let me fix it myself? I'm hurt."

"You charge too much," Annie said, setting her basket on the table.

Molly laughed, folding the shirt neatly. "Fair enough. What brings you here, then? Surely not just to admire my work?"

Annie sat on the stool beside the table, glancing around at the other seamstresses. Most were busy, too focused on their stitching to notice her. The workshop smelled of wool, cotton, and the faint scent of starch. It was a different world from the cobbler shop.

Molly leaned against the table. "You look better today."

Annie raised an eyebrow. "Do I?"

"You do," Molly said. "You're not scowling for once."

"I don't scowl."

Molly snorted. "You do. But right now, you don't. What changed?"

Annie hesitated and Molly nudged her. "Come on. You've got that look again."

"What look?"

"The one where you're thinking too much. Must I remind you that thinking is dangerous?"

Annie huffed a laugh. "Thinking is necessary."

"Necessary, maybe," Molly said, "but too much of it is bad for the soul." She tilted her head. "Tell me something good instead. A bit of gossip, maybe?"

Annie smirked. "I thought you didn't like gossip."

"I don't," Molly said, grinning. "But I do like stories. And there's always a story behind a bit of gossip."

Annie pretended to consider. "I did hear something interesting at the market."

Molly leaned closer. "Go on."

Annie lowered her voice. "Mr. Cartwright's daughter ran off."

Molly's eyes widened. "No!"

"With a baker's apprentice."

Molly clapped her hands. "Oh, I love this. Did they run far?"

"Far enough," Annie said. "They took the morning coach."

Molly grinned. "I bet her father is furious."

"Red as a beet, they said."

Molly laughed, shaking her head. "Good for her, I say. That man was awful. Always acting like no one in this town was worth his time."

Annie smirked. "Seems his daughter disagreed."

Molly wiped at her eyes, still smiling. "Oh, Annie, I've missed this."

Annie tilted her head. "Missed what?"

"You," Molly said. "Laughing. Talking like this."

Annie hesitated.

"You've been so serious lately," Molly went on. "I know you have your reasons, but it's nice to see you look..." She paused, searching for the word. "Lighter."

Annie exhaled. "It won't last."

"Maybe not," Molly said. "But for now, it's enough."

TOM

Rain pattered against the windows of the Fox and Hound, droplets racing down the glass in crooked paths. The pub was mostly empty now, the regular crowd having gone home for the night. Only a few men remained, gathered around a corner table far from the bar.

Tom Hartley set his empty mug down and leaned forward. "Thank you all for coming."

Jack Davidson nodded. "Not like we had much choice. Things can't go on as they are."

The other men around the table murmured in agreement. Billy sat beside his father, who looked better than he had in weeks, though his injured leg was still propped on a stool beside him. Robert Burns, a hulking man with hands like spades who worked in the loading bay, sat to Tom's left. Across from them, Owen Fletcher from the dye works stared into his ale.

"We need to be careful," Tom said, glancing toward the bar where the owner, Walter Reed, was wiping glasses with a cloth. "Reed's a good man, but walls have ears."

"Especially when Drake has men in every tavern," Billy's father muttered.

Tom looked at each man in turn. "You all know why we're here. Drake's got his fingers in every part of this town now. The mill, the properties, the loans. He's squeezing harder every day."

"What can we do about it?" Fletcher asked. "He's got friends in high places. We're just workers."

"We gather proof," Tom said simply. "Every bit of it we can find."

Robert Burns let out a low whistle. "You're talking about building a case against him? That's madness, Tom. Men who cross Drake end up broken or gone."

"What's the alternative?" Tom asked. "Let him take everything? Watch our neighbors lose their homes? See more men like Billy's father injured because Drake cuts corners on safety?"

Davidson shifted in his seat. "Tom's right. But Burns is right too. It's a risk."

Jack, who had been silent, finally spoke. "A man with nothing left to lose has nothing left to fear." His missing fingers tapped against the table in a rhythm. "I'm in. I've lost too much already to back down now."

"Me too," Billy said.

His father placed a hand on his shoulder. "You need to think of your mother and sisters, son."

"I am thinking of them," Billy insisted. "What happens when the next payment comes due? Or when Drake decides he wants Maggie working in his factory? We can't keep running."

Tom watched the others at the table, letting them work it through.

"What exactly would we need to do?" Fletcher asked.

Tom leaned back in his chair. "Keep your ears open. Watch who meets with Drake or his men. Write down names, dates, amounts. Anything about property sales or loans or workers who disappeared. We'll meet again in a week and put it all together."

"And then what?" Burns asked.

"We take it to someone who can use it. The

THE COBBLER'S DAUGHTER

county magistrate, maybe. Someone outside Drake's reach."

Davidson shook his head. "That's assuming anyone is beyond his reach."

"There has to be someone," Tom insisted. "Drake may own this town, but he doesn't own the whole country."

The men fell silent, each lost in thought. The rain grew heavier outside, drumming against the roof.

"I'll do it," Burns said finally, his large fist clenching on the table. "My brother took one of Drake's loans last year. Haven't seen him since March. Wife says he's working in the northern mines to pay it off, but he wouldn't leave his children for this long by choice."

Fletcher nodded too. "Count me in."

One by one, the others agreed, even Davidson. When they had all spoken, Tom pulled out a small notebook from his pocket.

"Write down what you already know," he said, tearing out pages and passing them around with a stub of pencil. "Names, dates, anything you can remember. We'll build from there."

For the next hour, the men worked and when they finished, Tom collected the papers and tucked them carefully into his jacket.

"One week," he said. "Same time. Be careful who you talk to. And if anyone asks what we're doing…"

"We're forming a burial society," Jack cut in with a wry smile. "Planning for our own funerals."

Fletcher let out a bark of laughter. "Not far from the truth, is it?"

They left in pairs, spacing their departures. Tom was the last to leave, nodding to Reed as he stepped out into the rain, pulling his collar up against the chill.

The streets were dark and empty, puddles reflecting the few gas lamps that still burned. Tom walked quickly, his mind working through what they'd learned. Burns' brother vanished to the northern mines. Fletcher's cousin, whose shop had mysteriously burned down after he refused to sell to one of Drake's men. Davidson's neighbor, whose daughter now worked fourteen hours a day in Drake's cotton mill to pay off her father's debt.

Drake didn't just want money. He wanted control. Complete control of the town and everyone in it.

Tom turned down the narrow lane that led to his mother's cottage. Despite the late hour, a light still burned in the window. He knocked softly, not wanting to wake the neighbors.

The door opened at once. Sarah Hartley stood in the doorway, her gray hair loose around her shoulders, a shawl pulled tight around her thin frame.

"You're soaked through," she said, pulling him inside. "Come by the fire."

The cottage was small but warm, a fire burning low in the hearth. Everything was neat and in its place, just as his father had always insisted. Thomas Hartley might be five years in the grave, but his presence still filled the little home he'd built with his own hands.

"You waited up," Tom said, hanging his wet coat by the door.

"Of course I did." His mother moved to the kitchen and returned with a cup of tea. "How was your meeting?"

Tom took the cup gratefully. "Good. Better than I expected. We have seven men willing to help gather information on Drake."

His mother nodded, sitting in her chair by the fire. "Be careful, Tom. Drake's not a man to cross lightly."

"I know." Tom sat across from her, stretching his legs toward the warmth. "But someone has to stand up to him. You've seen what's happening in town."

"I have." She studied his face in the firelight. "This

isn't just about the town, though, is it? It's about the Sutherlands too."

Tom looked down at his cup. "Their shop is part of it. Drake wants the whole block."

"And the girl is part of it too, I think." His mother's eyes crinkled at the corners.

"Annie has nothing to do with this," Tom protested, though he could feel his neck warming.

His mother laughed softly. "Tom Hartley, I've known you since before you drew breath. You think I don't see how you look at her? How you find every excuse to visit that shop?"

Tom ran a hand through his damp hair. "She needs help, Ma. Her father's been sick, and Drake's got his claws in them with that loan."

"Mmm." His mother sipped her tea. "And I suppose you look at every person who needs help the way you look at Annie Sutherland?"

Tom stayed silent, knowing there was no point denying it.

"Well?" his mother pressed. "What do you intend to do about it?"

"Do about what?"

"About Annie, of course." She set her cup down. "You care for the girl. That much is plain to see."

"It doesn't matter how I feel," Tom said. "She's

proud, Ma. Too proud to accept help, let alone... anything else."

"Ah, so you have thought about 'anything else,'" his mother said with a knowing smile.

Tom felt his face flush fully now. "Ma..."

"She reminds me of myself at that age," his mother continued, ignoring his embarrassment. "I turned your father away three times before I said yes. He used to climb up on our roof and fix the leaks just to have an excuse to see me."

"Is that why you never let me fix your roof?" Tom asked, seizing the chance to change the subject. "Hoping for a visit from a suitor?"

His mother swatted his arm. "Don't be cheeky. The roof needs fixing because it's old, same as me."

"I'll come by tomorrow and take care of it," Tom promised.

"Good." She settled back in her chair. "Now, about Annie Sutherland."

Tom groaned. "There's nothing to talk about."

"There's plenty to talk about. She's not as indifferent as she pretends."

Hope stirred in Tom's chest, but he tamped it down. "Even if that's true, now's not the time. Not with everything happening with Drake."

His mother reached out and patted his hand.

"Sometimes trouble is exactly when people find each other, Tom. Your father and I met during the worst flood this town ever saw. He pulled me from the river when my family's cart overturned."

Tom had heard the story many times, but he let her tell it again, watching the memories soften her face.

"The point is," she concluded, "don't wait for the perfect time. There isn't one. If you care for the girl, tell her."

"It's not that simple."

"Of course it is." His mother stood and moved to the small kitchen area. "Are you hungry? I saved you some stew."

Tom realized he was starving. "Yes, please."

She ladled stew into a bowl and brought it to him with a chunk of bread. Tom ate while she bustled around the cottage, straightening things that didn't need straightening.

"You know," she said casually as she folded a blanket, "Silas Drake came calling here once."

Tom stopped with his spoon halfway to his mouth. "Drake? Here?"

His mother nodded. "About a year after your father died. He offered to buy the cottage for twice what it was worth."

"Why would he want this place?" Tom asked, looking around the small room.

"It wasn't the cottage he wanted." His mother's voice was matter of fact. "It was me."

Tom set his bowl down with a thunk. "What?"

"Oh, he dressed it up nicely. Said a widow like me shouldn't have to work so hard. Said he could provide a comfortable life." She sniffed. "I told him I was perfectly capable of providing for myself."

"And he backed down?" Tom couldn't imagine Drake accepting rejection so easily.

"Not at first." His mother sat back down. "He kept coming back. Kept offering more money. Then he started making threats about having the property taxes reassessed. A woman living alone might find it hard to protect herself from 'accidents.'"

Tom felt a cold anger building in his chest. "He threatened you? Why didn't you tell me?"

"What could you have done? You were nineteen, working dawn to dusk at the mill." She waved a hand dismissively. "Besides, Reverend Clarke happened to call on me one day while Drake was here. After that, Drake never came back."

"The Reverend scared him off?" Tom couldn't quite believe it.

His mother smiled. "Not directly. But suddenly

the whole town knew Drake was pressuring a widow. Bad for his reputation, I suppose. He was still building his business then, still cared what people thought." Her smile faded. "He's beyond caring now."

Tom finished his stew in silence, thinking about what his mother had told him.

"I should go," Tom said finally, standing. "It's late, and I have an early shift."

His mother walked him to the door. "Come by tomorrow for the roof. And Tom..." She touched his arm. "Be careful. Drake remembers those who cross him. And he has a long reach."

"I'll be careful," Tom promised, kissing her cheek. "Lock the door behind me."

The rain had stopped, leaving the streets slick and shining in the moonlight. Tom walked quickly, his thoughts moving between the meeting, his mother's story, and Annie. Always back to Annie.

His mother was right about one thing—he did look at Annie differently. He couldn't help it. From the first moment he'd properly met her, something about her had called to him. Her pride, her determination, the way she cared for her father. The rare moments when she let down her guard and showed the person beneath the stubborn exterior.

He was so lost in thought that he almost walked straight past his boarding house. As he turned toward the steps, a figure stepped out from the shadows of the building next door.

"Hartley."

Tom tensed, ready for trouble, then relaxed slightly as he recognized Jenkins, the mill clerk. "Jenkins. What are you doing here?"

Jenkins glanced nervously up and down the street. "I need to talk to you. Not here."

Tom studied the man. Jenkins had worked at the mill for years, keeping the wage books and handling the paperwork. He wasn't one of Drake's men, as far as Tom knew, but he wasn't one to rock the boat either.

"Come up, then," Tom said, unlocking the front door of the boarding house. "Quietly, though. Mrs. Briggs doesn't like visitors after ten."

They climbed the stairs silently and entered Tom's small room. It was neat but spare, a narrow bed, a washstand, a chair, and a small table. Tom lit the lamp and turned to face Jenkins.

"What's this about?" he asked, keeping his voice low.

Jenkins removed his hat, revealing thinning hair

plastered to his skull with sweat despite the cool night. "I know what you're doing, Hartley."

Tom kept his face neutral. "And what's that?"

"Gathering information on Drake. On his loans, his businesses." Jenkins twisted his hat in his hands. "I saw you all at the Fox and Hound tonight."

Tom tensed again. "If Drake sent you…"

"He didn't," Jenkins cut in. "I came on my own. To give you this." He reached into his coat and pulled out a small, leather-bound book. "It's a record. Of everything Drake's done at the mill."

Tom took the book cautiously and opened it. It was page after page of neat columns, dates, names, amounts. Workers who had taken loans, when they had disappeared, where they had been sent. Safety violations that had been covered up. Bribes paid to inspectors.

"Why are you giving me this?" Tom asked, looking up from the pages.

Jenkins sank into the room's only chair, suddenly looking older. "My nephew, Samuel. He took a loan from Drake two years ago. Just five pounds to buy medicine for his mother, my sister. When he couldn't pay it back fast enough, Drake sent him to work in the coal mines up north. Said the wages were better, he could pay it off quicker."

"And did he?"

Jenkins shook his head. "Mine collapse. Six months ago. Twenty men dead, including Samuel. Drake sent my sister a letter saying Samuel still owed three pounds on his debt, and now she'd have to pay it."

"That's…" Tom couldn't find the words.

"It's what he does," Jenkins said flatly. "He owns people. Body and soul. I started keeping records after Samuel died. Thought maybe someday I'd find a way to use them."

"Why now?" Tom asked. "Why give this to me?"

"Because you're fighting back." Jenkins looked up, his eyes tired. "I'm not brave enough to do it myself. Too scared of losing my position. But I can help someone who is."

Tom closed the book, feeling the weight of it in his hands. "This is dangerous, Jenkins. If Drake finds out…"

"I know." Jenkins stood up. "That's why I made a copy. The original is hidden. If anything happens to me, my sister knows where to find it."

Tom nodded, impressed by the clerk's foresight. "Thank you. This will help."

Jenkins put his hat back on. "There's one more thing you should know. Drake's planning something big. I overheard him talking with Harding yesterday. They're going to lay off another thirty men next month, just before buying up the rest of High Street."

"The rest of... that includes the Sutherlands' shop."

"Among others." Jenkins moved to the door. "Be careful, Hartley. Drake has men watching you. He knows you're getting close to the Sutherland girl."

Tom felt a chill that had nothing to do with the night air. "How do you know that?"

"Because he told Harding to make sure you're on the list for layoffs." Jenkins opened the door. "You're a marked man now."

With that, he slipped out, leaving Tom alone with the ledger and the knowledge that he had even less time than he'd thought.

Tom sat on the edge of his bed, opening the ledger again. Names leapt out at him. Men he knew, men he'd worked with. Some who had disappeared without explanation. Some who had been moved to more dangerous jobs. Some who had lost homes or shops.

And now Annie and her father were caught too. The thought of Drake targeting them, of Annie being forced to work in one of his factories, made Tom's blood run cold.

He tucked the ledger under his mattress and blew out the lamp. Sleep would be a long time coming tonight. Too much to think about. Too much to plan.

But one thing was certain, the fight against Drake was no longer just about the town or even about justice. It was personal now. Drake had threatened his mother, was targeting his job, and had plans for Annie's shop.

Tom stared into the darkness, making a silent promise to himself. Drake might have money and power and friends in high places. But Tom had something Drake would never understand.

He had people worth fighting for.

ANNIE

Annie held the boots wrapped in brown paper, tied with twine in a neat package. The morning sun warmed her back as she walked toward the west end of town, where the houses grew larger and the streets wider. She'd spent three days on Mr. Nazari's boots, crafting them with care from the finest leather she could afford. The order had come as a surprise, bank managers didn't typically seek out small cobbler shops when they could afford London-made footwear.

She turned onto Maple Lane, where trees lined both sides of the street, their new spring leaves casting dappled shadows on the cobblestones. The Nazari house stood halfway down, not as grand as some but still impressive with its redbrick front and polished brass knocker.

Annie smoothed her skirt, aware of her simple dress and worn shawl. Then she lifted the knocker and let it fall against the plate.

A maid in a crisp uniform opened the door. "Yes, miss?"

"I have a delivery for Mr. Nazari," Annie said, holding up the package. "From Sutherland's Cobbler Shop."

The maid nodded. "Please wait here."

The door closed, leaving Annie on the step. She shifted her weight from one foot to the other, uncomfortable in the quiet, wealthy street where she clearly didn't belong. A minute passed, then two. Just as she considered leaving the package with a note, the door opened again.

Mrs. Nazari herself stood in the doorway. She was a small woman with dark hair pinned neatly under a lace cap, her dress of fine blue wool far nicer than anything Annie had worn in years.

"Miss Sutherland," Mrs. Nazari said with a smile. "Please, come in."

Annie hesitated. "I just brought the boots for your husband, ma'am. I don't need to trouble you."

"No trouble at all." Mrs. Nazari held the door wider. "In fact, I hoped to have a word with you."

Curiosity overcame Annie's reluctance. She stepped into a hallway with polished wood floors and wallpaper imported from France. The scent of beeswax and lavender hung in the air.

"My husband is at the bank," Mrs. Nazari said, leading Annie toward the back of the house.

Annie handed over the package. "They should fit well. I followed the measurements exactly."

Mrs. Nazari set the package on a side table. "Would you care for tea, Miss Sutherland? I was just about to have some."

Annie looked down at her plain dress, feeling out of place among the fine furnishings. "Thank you, ma'am, but I should get back to the shop. My father..."

"Is much improved, I hear," Mrs. Nazari said. "News travels fast in a town this size. Please, just a cup of tea. There are matters I think might interest you."

Something in her tone made Annie pause. "What matters?"

Mrs. Nazari glanced toward the hallway, then lowered her voice. "Matters concerning Silas Drake."

The name sent a chill through Annie. She

nodded. "Then I'd be happy to stay for tea."

Mrs. Nazari led her to a morning room at the back of the house, sunny and pleasant with windows overlooking a small garden. She rang a bell, and the maid appeared moments later.

"Tea, please, Martha. And some of those almond cakes."

When the maid had gone, Mrs. Nazari gestured to a chair. "Please, sit. Make yourself comfortable."

Annie sat on the edge of the chair, her back straight. "You mentioned Mr. Drake, ma'am?"

Mrs. Nazari settled into her own chair. "Yes, but let's wait for the tea. Walls have ears, as they say, even in one's own home these days."

They spoke of inconsequential things until the maid returned with a tray. Mrs. Nazari thanked her and waited until the door closed behind her.

"Sugar?" she asked, lifting the pot.

"No, thank you," Annie replied. "Just milk."

Mrs. Nazari prepared the tea, then sat back with her cup. "Miss Sutherland, I'll speak plainly. My husband and I are concerned about Mr. Drake's influence in this town."

Annie took a sip of tea. "Many people share that concern."

"Yes, but few are in a position to know the extent

of it." Mrs. Nazari leaned forward. "My husband is the manager of the bank, as you know. He sees the financial dealings of most businesses in town, including Mr. Drake's."

"I thought bankers kept such matters private," Annie said cautiously.

"They do. Absolutely." Mrs. Nazari set her cup down. "Which is why what I'm about to tell you must remain between us."

Annie nodded. "Of course."

Mrs. Nazari took a breath. "Mr. Drake is planning to purchase the entire block of buildings on High Street that includes your shop."

The teacup trembled in Annie's hand. "The whole block? But why?"

"To demolish it. He plans to build a large department store selling factory-made goods. Boots, clothing, household items, all at prices small shops like yours can't possibly match."

Annie set her cup down before she spilled it. "How do you know this?"

"I saw the plans on my husband's desk. Drake brought them to the bank last week, seeking financing for the project." Mrs. Nazari's face grew troubled. "He already owns three of the buildings on your block. Yours is one of the few remaining."

"Through Mr. Baxter?" Annie asked, remembering the increased rent.

Mrs. Nazari nodded. "Peter Baxter sold most of his properties to Drake six months ago but continues to manage them. The rent increases, and the new strict rules are all Drake's doing."

"Surely your husband wouldn't approve."

Mrs. Nazari's expression hardened. "My husband is a good man caught in a difficult position. The bank's board of directors includes two of Drake's closest associates. If he openly opposes Drake's plans, he could lose his position."

She stood and walked to a small desk in the corner of the room. From a drawer, she removed a folder tied with ribbon.

"These are copies of loan documents, property transfers, and correspondence regarding Drake's plans for High Street." She held out the folder. "There are names, dates, amounts, everything you might need to prove what he's doing."

Annie stared at the folder. "If Mr. Drake discovered you shared these..."

"He would ruin us," Mrs. Nazari said simply. "My husband would lose his position. We would lose our home. Perhaps worse."

"Then why take the risk?"

Mrs. Nazari smiled sadly. "Because some things matter more than comfort or security. The people of this town matter. Small shops like yours matter." She pressed the folder into Annie's hands. "Take it. Use it however you can."

Annie clutched the folder, overwhelmed by the risk this woman was taking. "Thank you. I don't know what to say."

"Say you'll fight," Mrs. Nazari replied. "Not just for your shop, but for everyone Drake has trapped in his schemes."

Annie nodded, tucking the folder into her bag. "I will."

They finished their tea in silence, both aware of the weight of what had just passed between them. When Annie rose to leave, Mrs. Nazari walked her to the door.

"Be careful, Miss Sutherland," she said softly.

"I will," Annie promised.

The walk back to High Street seemed longer somehow, and when she turned onto High Street, she stopped short. A group of men stood outside her shop, some shifting impatiently, others talking among themselves. For a moment, fear gripped her, had Drake sent them? Had he somehow learned of her visit to Mrs. Nazari?

Then she recognized one of the men. It was Samuel Reed, who worked at the cotton mill. Beside him stood Walter Cole from the dye works, and behind them, three other men she'd seen around town but couldn't name.

She approached cautiously. "Good morning, gentlemen. Can I help you?"

Samuel turned, his face brightening. "Miss Sutherland! We were hoping your shop was open."

"It is," Annie said, still confused. "My father should be inside."

"Thank goodness," Walter said. "I've been walking on a broken heel for two days. Miss Peters at the sewing shop said you could fix them quick and proper."

"Miss Peters?" Annie repeated. "Molly?"

"That's right," Samuel nodded. "She told half the mill about your father's work. Said there wasn't a pair of boots in town he couldn't mend."

Understanding dawned. "Of course. Please, come in."

Annie unlocked the door, ushering the men inside. To her surprise, her father was already at the workbench, a boot in his hands and a smile on his face.

"Ah, there you are, girl," he called. "We've got customers waiting."

The shop looked different, cleaner, more organized. The leather pieces were neatly stacked, tools arranged in order on the wall. Even the windows seemed brighter, as if they'd been washed.

"I see that," Annie said, setting her bag aside. "Let me wash up and I'll help."

By midday, they had more orders than they'd seen in months. Annie worked through lunch, too busy to stop. Her father insisted on staying at the bench, though she made him take breaks to rest.

"Have you ever seen such a day?" he asked during one such break, sipping water from a cup. "Six pairs for repair and two orders for new boots."

"Never," Annie agreed, wiping her hands on her apron. "What happened while I was gone?"

Her father chuckled. "Molly Peters happened. She brought half a dozen women to look at my carved heels, then spread word at the mill that we were offering fair prices for quality work."

The bell above the door jingled, and Molly herself bustled in, her cheeks pink from hurrying.

"Did I miss them?" she asked. "The men from the mill?"

"Most of them," Annie said, moving to embrace

her friend. "Thank you, Molly."

Molly returned the hug. "Think nothing of it. That's what neighbors do." She stepped back to survey the shop. "My, you have been busy! Look at all these boots waiting for repair!"

"Thanks to you," Annie's father said. "You're a blessing, Miss Peters."

Molly waved away the compliment. "Nonsense. I only told the truth—that the finest cobbler in the county was back at his bench and charging half what those factory boots cost."

She moved around the shop, examining the boots lined up for repair. "You'll need help with all this. Good thing I have the afternoon free."

"You don't have to..." Annie began.

"I want to," Molly insisted. "Besides, Mrs. Davis gave me the day off. She's visiting her sister in the next town." She untied her bonnet and hung it on a peg. "Now, what can I do?"

The sun was beginning to set when the last customer left. Annie locked the door behind him and leaned against it, suddenly aware of how tired she was.

"What a day," she said, pushing a strand of hair back from her face.

Molly nodded, flexing her fingers. "My hands

aren't used to leather work. Much tougher than cotton."

"You did wonderfully," Annie's father said. "Both of you." He stood from his bench, stretching his back. "I think I'll head upstairs for a rest before supper."

Annie watched him climb the stairs, and when the door to their living quarters closed behind him, she turned to Molly.

"I can't thank you enough," she said. "This...all of this...it's because of you."

Molly smiled. "It's because you and father make good boots and good repairs. All I did was remind people of that."

"Still," Annie insisted, "today would never have happened without you."

"Maybe not today," Molly conceded, "but it would have happened eventually. Quality speaks for itself." She reached for her bonnet. "I should get home. Mother will be wondering where I am."

After Molly left, Annie locked the door and moved to the small desk in the corner of the shop. She pulled out the account book and began calculating the day's earnings. Order after order, repair after repair, the numbers adding up to more than they'd made in the past two weeks combined.

She hid the folder in a hollow space beneath a floorboard under her workbench, a hiding place her father had created years ago for their most valuable tools. Then she went upstairs to prepare a simple supper to share with her father.

He was sitting by the window, looking out at the street below. "You should rest, girl," he said as she set the tray on the small table. "You've worked hard today."

"So have you," she replied, pouring tea for them both. "How do you feel?"

"Better than I have in months." He smiled, the lines around his eyes crinkling. "It feels good to be useful again."

When they finished, her father insisted on washing the dishes while Annie prepared for bed.

"Sleep well," he said, kissing her forehead as he had when she was a child. "Tomorrow will be another busy day."

Annie tried to sleep, but her mind refused to quiet. She tossed and turned, thinking of the folder hidden beneath the floorboard. Finally, she gave up. Pulling on her dress and shawl, she crept downstairs to the shop. Perhaps work would tire her enough for sleep.

She lit a single lamp, keeping the flame low so as

not to wake her father or alert anyone passing by that the shop was occupied at such a late hour. The boots from the day's orders sat in a neat row, waiting for repair. Annie selected one, a simple job that wouldn't require much thought, and settled at her bench.

A soft knock at the door startled her. She froze, needle poised mid-stitch. Who would come at this hour? Had Drake learned of her visit to Mrs. Nazari already?

The knock came again, gentle but insistent. Annie set down her work and moved to the door, peering through a crack in the curtains.

Tom Hartley stood outside, his cap in his hands, looking as tired as she felt. Relief flooded through her, followed by confusion. What was he doing here so late?

She unbolted the door and opened it just enough to speak. "Tom? Is something wrong?"

He looked surprised to see her. "Annie. I saw the light. I didn't expect... I was just passing by."

"Passing by at this hour?" she asked skeptically.

Tom ran a hand through his hair. "I couldn't sleep. Thought a walk might help." He glanced past her into the shop. "You're working late."

"I couldn't sleep either," she admitted.

THE COBBLER'S DAUGHTER

They stood in silence for a moment, neither sure what to say next. Then Annie stepped back, opening the door wider.

"Would you like some tea?" she asked. "Since we're both awake anyway."

Tom hesitated, then nodded. "If it's not too much trouble."

Annie led him into the shop, closing and bolting the door behind him. "Sit. I'll put the kettle on."

While she heated water on the small stove in the corner, Tom wandered the shop, looking at the boots lined up for repair.

"Busy day?" he asked.

Annie nodded, measuring tea leaves into the pot. "Busiest in months. Molly sent half the mill our way."

"Good," Tom said. "That's good." He touched a pair of boots waiting for new soles. "Your father's work?"

"Yes. He's much better. He worked the whole day without tiring." The kettle began to whistle, and Annie quickly removed it from the heat, not wanting to wake her father. "The medicine helped. Truly."

She poured water over the leaves, the familiar scent of tea filling the small space between them. "It'll need to steep for a few minutes."

Tom nodded, taking a seat on the customer

bench. Annie sat across from him at her workbench, suddenly aware of the intimacy of the moment, the two of them alone in the lamplight, the rest of the world asleep.

"Sugar?"

"No, thank you."

She handed him a cup, their fingers brushing in the exchange. Neither acknowledged it, but Annie felt the touch like a spark against her skin.

"I visited Mrs. Nazari today," she said after a moment. "To deliver her husband's boots."

Tom blew on his tea, watching her over the rim of his cup. "Did she have news?"

Annie hesitated, unsure how much to share. But if she couldn't trust Tom, who could she trust? "She gave me documents to proof Drake's plans for High Street."

Tom's eyes widened. "What kind of plans?"

"He wants to buy the entire block. Tear down the buildings. Build a department store." Annie stared into her tea. "He already owns most of it through his associates."

"I know," Tom said. "Jenkins told me the same thing last night."

"What can we do?" Annie asked. "He's too powerful. We're just... we're nobody."

"That's not true," Tom said firmly. "You're not nobody, Annie. None of us are. And there are more of us than there are of him."

Annie wanted to believe him. Wanted to think they stood a chance against Drake and his money and connections. But the weight of their debt pressed down on her, cold and real.

"Even if that's true," she said, "he still holds our loan. He can take the shop whenever he wants."

"Not if we stop him," Tom insisted. "Not if we fight back."

Annie looked up at him, at the determination in his face despite the shadows of exhaustion under his eyes. "How?"

Tom set his cup down. "We gather proof and build a case against him. Take it to someone with the power to do something about it."

"Who? The magistrate? The mayor? They're all Drake's friends."

"Not all of them." Tom leaned forward. "There are decent men in this town. And beyond it. The county judge isn't in Drake's pocket, not yet anyway."

Annie wanted to believe him. "It seems impossible."

"Most important things do," Tom said with a small smile. "But that doesn't mean we shouldn't try."

They fell silent, drinking their tea.

"My father loves this shop," Annie said suddenly. "Even more than my mother, I think. She used to tease him about it."

Tom looked up, surprised by the personal turn. "You never talk about your mother."

"No," Annie agreed. "It still hurts, sometimes."

"I understand," Tom said softly. "I feel the same way about my father."

Annie studied him in the lamplight. "What was he like?"

Tom traced the rim of his cup with his finger. "He was a carpenter. The best I've ever known. He could turn a piece of wood into anything you could imagine."

"Is that where you learned?" Annie asked. "I've seen the boxes you carved for my father."

Tom nodded. "He taught me everything I know. Used to say a man's hands should be able to create something worthwhile." He looked down at his own hands, calloused from work at the mill. "Not sure I've lived up to that."

"You have," Annie said softly. "Those boxes brought my father joy when he needed it most."

Tom smiled, a genuine smile that transformed his tired face. "He was working on a house when it happened. The framework collapsed. He pushed another man out of the way but couldn't save himself."

"I'm sorry," Annie said. "How old were you?"

"Seventeen. Old enough to work, young enough to still need him." Tom shook his head. "What about your mother?"

"Fever," Annie replied. "I was fourteen. She got sick in the spring. By summer, she was gone." The memories were still sharp, even after all these years. "My father was never the same after."

"Grief changes people," Tom said.

"Yes," Annie agreed.

As the first light of dawn crept through the windows, Tom stood reluctantly. "I should go. My shift starts in an hour."

Annie nodded, gathering their cups. "Thank you for the company. It was... nice, not to be alone with my thoughts."

Tom moved toward the door, then stopped. "I should go," he said again, his voice lower. "But I find I don't want to."

The simple confession hung in the air between them. Annie set the cups down and walked to where he stood, her heart beating faster with each step.

"I understand," she said softly. "I don't want you to go either."

She reached for the bolt on the door, her hand brushing against his. This time, instead of pulling away, she let her fingers curl around his, squeezing gently.

Tom looked down at their joined hands, then back at her face. The morning light cast a golden glow across his features, softening the lines of worry etched there.

"Annie," he said, her name almost a question.

She released his hand to slide the bolt open, but the brief contact lingered like warmth on her skin. "Be careful today," she said.

"You too," Tom replied, putting his cap on. "Don't go anywhere alone if you can help it."

As he stepped outside into the morning air, Annie felt fear for what lay ahead, determination to fight, and beneath it all, something new and fragile taking root in her heart.

She closed the door behind him, resting her forehead against the cool wood for a moment. Then she straightened her shoulders and turned back to the shop. There was work to be done, and for the first time in a long while, reasons to hope.

TOM

Steam hissed from pipes overhead, turning the air thick and wet. Tom wiped sweat from his forehead with his sleeve, though it did little good. His shirt had been soaked through within minutes of entering the boiler room, and three hours into his shift, every inch of him dripped with moisture.

The heat pressed in from all sides, a living thing with weight and force. Men moved through the haze like ghosts, their faces black with coal dust, their movements slow and careful. One wrong step, one moment of distraction, and the boilers could take a finger, a hand, or worse.

Tom shoveled coal into the hungry mouth of boiler three, his muscles burning with the effort. The pile never seemed to diminish, no matter how much they fed into the flames. The mill demanded more steam, more power, more production.

"Hartley!" A voice called. Davidson appeared from the steam, his face lined with exhaustion. "Your turn on the gauges."

Tom nodded, handing over his shovel. The men rotated tasks throughout the shift to prevent collapse from the heat. Gauge duty was supposedly easier, but it carried its own burden. If a man missed a rising pressure level or a failing valve, people died.

He moved to the control panel, wiping his hands on his trousers before checking each gauge in turn. The heat was worse here, so close to the boilers themselves. Tom squinted through the steam, making sure each needle sat in the safe zone.

Boiler one: normal. Boiler two: normal. Boiler three...

Tom frowned, tapping the glass. The pressure gauge for boiler three showed higher than usual, the needle edging toward the red. He checked the release valve, which should have been venting excess pressure automatically. It looked wrong somehow, the metal discolored around the edges.

"Stevens," Tom called to the supervisor, a thick-necked man who stood near the stairs. "Boiler three is running hot."

Stevens hardly glanced up from his clipboard. "Keep an eye on it."

"The release valve isn't working properly," Tom insisted, pointing to the gauge. "Look at the needle."

Stevens sighed heavily, as if Tom had asked him to move a mountain instead of walk ten feet. He stomped over, glanced at the gauge, and shrugged. "It's within limits."

"Barely," Tom argued. "And the valve looks wrong. The metal's discolored. It needs maintenance."

"Maintenance costs money," Stevens replied flatly. "And time. We're behind schedule as it is."

Tom stared at him in disbelief. "If that valve fails, the whole boiler could go. People will die."

"Don't be dramatic, Hartley." Stevens turned away. "Keep shoveling. That's what you're paid for."

Tom grabbed his arm. "I'm not leaving this post until that valve is fixed."

Stevens' face darkened. "You'll do as you're told, or you'll find yourself without a job."

"Better without a job than dead," Tom replied evenly.

Men nearby had stopped working, watching the

confrontation. Stevens looked around, aware of the audience.

"Get back to work!" he barked. "All of you!"

No one moved. Davidson stepped forward, his shovel still in hand. "Tom's right. That valve needs looking at."

Stevens' jaw worked, his face turning red beneath the coal dust. More men gathered, forming a silent wall of support behind Tom and Davidson.

"Fine," Stevens spat. "Wilson, get up here with your toolbox."

A thin man with gnarled hands hurried forward, carrying a metal box of tools. He immediately set to work on the valve, muttering under his breath.

"The rest of you, back to your stations," Stevens ordered. "Show's over."

The men dispersed slowly, reluctantly. Tom stayed by the gauge, watching Wilson work. Davidson remained too.

"This is the second one this month," Wilson said quietly as he loosened bolts on the valve housing. "'Tis getting worse, not better."

Tom leaned closer. "What do you mean?"

Wilson glanced toward Stevens, making sure he wasn't listening. "Maintenance requests keep getting denied because the parts ordered but never arriving and the inspections scheduled then canceled."

Davidson nodded. "Been that way since Drake started investing in the mill."

Wilson removed the valve cover and whistled softly. "Look at that."

Tom peered into the mechanism. Even with his limited knowledge of boilers, he could see something was very wrong. The spring inside the valve had been compressed far beyond its normal position, held in place by what looked like a small metal wedge.

"Someone did that on purpose," Davidson said, his voice barely audible over the machinery. "That's not wear and tear."

Wilson nodded grimly, already working to remove the wedge and replace the spring. "Happens more than you'd think. Especially in sections where men have been complaining."

A chill ran through Tom despite the heat. "You're saying someone's tampering with the equipment? Deliberately causing failures?"

Wilson didn't look up from his work. "I'm not saying anything. Just fixing a valve."

But Davidson met Tom's eyes. "Accidents

increase when workers complain too much," he said quietly.

Tom watched as Wilson completed the repair. He'd known Drake was ruthless in business, that he used debt and fear to control people. But this was different. This was risking dozens of lives, to silence dissent and increase profits.

"There," Wilson said, replacing the cover. "Should hold now. But keep an eye on it. And watch your back, Hartley. Standing up to Stevens like that puts a target on you."

The rest of the shift passed without incident, when the bell finally rang signaling the end of the shift, Tom's muscles ached with exhaustion.

Instead of turning toward his boarding house, Tom headed for the town hall. The records office would still be open for another hour. If he was going to fight Drake, he needed to understand exactly what he was up against.

The town hall stood in the center of the main square, its brick facade and columns designed to inspire confidence in local government. Tom climbed the steps, his body protesting every movement after the punishing boiler room shift.

Inside, the marble floors echoed with his footsteps. Most offices were closed at this hour, but light shone from under the door marked "Town Records and Archives." Tom knocked once, then entered.

The room smelled of paper and dust. Shelves lined the walls, filled with leather-bound volumes and stacks of documents. A single desk sat near the window, where a clerk in a green eyeshade peered at Tom over the top of his spectacles.

"We're closing soon," the clerk said by way of greeting.

"I'll be quick," Tom replied, approaching the desk. "I need to see property records for High Street. And any recent transfers of ownership for buildings in town."

The clerk's eyebrows rose. "That's quite a broad request. Those records are organized by address and date. You'd need to be more specific."

"The last six months, then," Tom said. "Starting with High Street, particularly the block containing Sutherland's Cobbler Shop."

"Are you a solicitor?" the clerk asked, making no move to help.

"No," Tom admitted. "Just a concerned citizen."

The clerk smiled thinly. "I'm afraid property records are only available to property owners, legal representatives, or town officials. Unless you fall into one of those categories..."

Tom bit back his frustration. "Look, Mr...."

"Finch. Harold Finch."

"Mr. Finch. These are public records. I have a right to see them."

Finch adjusted his spectacles. "The records are indeed public, but access is still regulated. I need to know your business with them."

"I'm researching property ownership patterns in town," Tom said, choosing his words carefully. "For a community project."

Finch looked unconvinced. "What sort of community project requires examining property transfers?"

Before Tom could answer, the door opened behind him. He turned to see Reverend Clarke entering the office, a folder tucked under his arm.

"Ah, Mr. Hartley," the Reverend said with a smile. "What brings you here this evening?"

Tom seized the opportunity. "Reverend Clarke. I was just explaining to Mr. Finch about our church committee's interest in property ownership patterns."

The Reverend's eyebrows rose slightly, but he caught on quickly. "Yes, indeed. Part of our community welfare initiative." He turned to Finch. "I trust you can assist Mr. Hartley? He's acting on behalf of the church."

Finch's demeanor changed immediately. "Of course, Reverend. Happy to help." He stood, smoothing his waistcoat. "The High Street records, you said? I'll fetch them directly."

As Finch disappeared into the stacks of documents, the Reverend gave Tom a questioning look.

"Church committee?" he asked quietly.

Tom had the grace to look abashed. "Forgive the lie, Reverend. But I need those records. It's important."

Reverend Clarke studied him for a moment, then nodded. "This is about Drake, isn't it?"

Tom stared at him, surprised. "You know?"

"I see the results every day," the Reverend said.

"It's worse than that," Tom said, lowering his voice. "There's evidence he's deliberately causing accidents at the mill and tampering with equipment to target workers who speak out."

The Reverend's face grew grave. "These are serious allegations, Tom."

"I know. That's why I need proof."

Finch returned, carrying several large ledgers. "Here we are. Property transfers for High Street and surrounding areas, going back one year." He set them on the desk. "Anything else?"

"Records of property disputes brought before the magistrate," Tom said. "Over the same period."

Finch hesitated, glancing between Tom and the Reverend. "That would be in the judicial records. I'm not certain I have authority..."

"I'm sure it won't be a problem," Reverend Clarke said smoothly. "After all, court proceedings are public record."

Finch nodded reluctantly. "Very well. I'll see what I can find."

As he disappeared again, Tom opened the first ledger, quickly scanning the entries. He pulled out a small notebook and began making notes.

"What exactly are you looking for?" the Reverend asked, peering over his shoulder.

"Patterns," Tom replied. "Properties changing hands multiple times in short periods. The same buyers appearing over and over. Especially anyone connected to Drake."

Together, they worked through the ledgers. The Reverend proved to have an excellent memory for names and connections, identifying several of Drake's known associates among the buyers.

"Martin Walsh," he said, pointing to one

entry. "He's Drake's brother-in-law. And here, William Hodge manages one of Drake's warehouses."

Finch returned with another ledger. "Court records. Property disputes brought before Magistrate Phillips in the past six months."

Tom flipped it open, scanning the cases. There weren't many, only a dozen or so, but something jumped out immediately.

"Look at this," he said to the Reverend. "Every case where Drake or one of his associates was involved, the magistrate ruled in their favor. Every single one."

The Reverend frowned. "That seems unlikely to be mere coincidence."

"And here," Tom continued, pointing to a recent entry. "Three eviction orders for High Street, all signed last week. These shops are still operating. They don't even know they're about to lose their premises."

"One of those must be the Sutherland shop," the Reverend said.

Tom checked the addresses. "No, not yet. But these are on the same block. He's working his way down."

"This goes beyond simple business," the Reverend

said at last. "This is a deliberate effort to control the town itself."

Tom nodded grimly. "And the town magistrate is helping him do it."

The clock on the wall chimed, indicating the hour. Finch looked up from his desk, where he'd been pretending not to listen to their conversation.

"Gentlemen, I must close the office now."

"Of course," Tom said, gathering his notes. "Thank you for your assistance."

As they prepared to leave, the door opened once more. A tall man in an expensive coat entered, his silver-topped cane tapping against the marble floor. Tom recognized him immediately: Magistrate Phillips, a thin man with hooded eyes and a permanent expression of mild distaste.

"Reverend Clarke," Phillips said, nodding coolly. "Working late, I see."

"Just finishing some research, Magistrate," the Reverend replied. "Mr. Hartley has been kind enough to assist me."

Phillips turned his gaze to Tom, taking in his work clothes and coal-stained hands. "Hartley? From the cotton mill, if I'm not mistaken."

"Yes, sir," Tom said, meeting his gaze steadily.

"Interesting," Phillips murmured. "I wouldn't

have thought mill work left much time for... research." His eyes flicked to the ledgers still open on the desk, then back to Tom. "Curiosity can be dangerous in these times, young man. Especially when it extends beyond one's proper sphere."

The words were delivered mildly, almost pleasantly, but the threat behind them was clear. Tom felt anger rise in his chest, but before he could respond, Reverend Clarke stepped forward.

"So is silence in the face of injustice, Magistrate," he said firmly. "As our Lord himself demonstrated when he drove the money-changers from the temple."

Phillips' mouth tightened. "Biblical allusions, Reverend? How... predictable. I hope your sermon this Sunday focuses more on rendering unto Caesar what is Caesar's, and less on... controversial interpretations."

"I preach as my conscience and God's word direct me," the Reverend replied. "As I always have."

The two men stared at each other for a long moment. Finally, Phillips smiled thinly and stepped aside.

"Don't let me keep you. Good evening, gentlemen."

Tom and the Reverend moved past him toward the door. As they reached it, Phillips spoke again.

"Mr. Hartley. I understand you're acquainted with the Sutherland girl. The cobbler's daughter."

Tom stopped, turning slowly. "I know Miss Sutherland, yes."

Phillips tapped his cane thoughtfully against the floor. "A pretty young woman. It would be a shame if her father's business encountered... difficulties. The market is so changeable these days."

Tom felt his hands curl into fists. "Good night, Magistrate,"

Outside, the evening air had cooled considerably. Tom took several deep breaths, trying to calm his racing heart.

The Reverend glanced at his pocket watch. "I must get back to the church. We're preparing for the spring social tomorrow evening."

Tom had forgotten all about the social. The church held one every year to raise funds for families in need. This year, it was dedicated to those affected by the mine collapse that had killed Jenkins' nephew and so many others.

"Will you attend?" the Reverend asked.

Tom hadn't planned to. Social gatherings weren't

his usual preference, especially when he was working double shifts.

"Yes," he said. "I'll be there."

The Reverend smiled. "Good. A little normalcy might do us all good in these troubled times." He clapped Tom on the shoulder. "Get some rest, my friend. You look exhausted."

They parted ways, the Reverend heading toward the church while Tom turned toward his boarding house. But he didn't go directly home. Instead, he made a detour past High Street, past the darkened windows of Sutherland's Cobbler Shop.

A light still burned in the upstairs window, Annie's room. Tom stood for a moment, watching the warm glow. Was she safe? Would Drake target her next, knowing Tom cared for her?

The thought sent a chill through him. He needed to warn her, to explain what he'd discovered. But not tonight. Not when Phillips might have men watching. Tomorrow, at the social, they could speak more freely.

* * *

The church hall was transformed. Paper lanterns hung from the rafters, casting a warm glow over the space. Tables lined the walls, laden with food and drink donated by parishioners. At one end, a small group of musicians played, their tunes bright and cheerful.

Tom stood near the entrance, feeling out of place despite his best clothes, a clean shirt, his only pair of trousers without patches, and his father's old jacket, a bit tight in the shoulders but well-made. People filled the hall, talking, laughing, a brief respite from the hardships of daily life.

"Tom Hartley, as I live and breathe." Mrs. Reed, the pub owner's wife, approached with a smile. "I didn't expect to see you here."

"Mrs. Reed," Tom nodded politely. "It's for a good cause."

"Indeed, it is. Those poor families from the mine disaster..." She shook her head. "Will you have some punch? I made it myself."

Tom accepted a cup, scanning the room as he sipped. He recognized many faces, mill workers, shopkeepers, farmers from outside town. Reverend Clarke moved among them, stopping to chat with each group, his wife at his side.

And then he saw her.

Annie stood near the refreshment table with Molly, wearing a dress Tom had never seen before. It was dark blue with a modest neckline. but on her, it looked elegant. Her hair was arranged differently too, styled in a way that framed her face, emphasizing her fine features.

Tom couldn't look away. She was laughing at something Molly had said. It was a side of Annie he rarely saw. She was carefree, unburdened by worry, if only for a moment.

"You might as well go talk to her," a voice said beside him. "Staring won't accomplish much."

Tom turned to find Jack Davidson grinning at him, a cup of punch in his gnarled hand.

"I don't know what you mean," Tom protested weakly.

Jack laughed. "Sure you don't. You've only been making eyes at the Sutherland girl for months now."

Tom felt his face warm. "Is it that obvious?"

"To everyone but her, apparently," Jack replied. "Go on. Ask her to dance. What's the worst that could happen?"

"She could say no," Tom muttered.

"Then you'd be right where you are now," Jack pointed out reasonably. "But she won't."

"How can you be so sure?"

Jack's eyes twinkled. "Because she's been looking

for you since she arrived. Kept glancing at the door every time it opened."

Hope flared in Tom's chest. "Really?"

"Really." Jack gave him a gentle push. "Now go, before someone else asks her first."

Tom handed his empty cup to Jack and made his way across the room, weaving between groups of chatting parishioners. His heart pounded in his chest, louder than the music playing from the corner.

Annie saw him when he was halfway to her. Their eyes met across the room, and for a moment, everyone else seemed to fade into the background. She smiled a small, private smile that made Tom's steps falter.

He reached her at last, suddenly aware of his rough hands and worn clothes beside her simple elegance.

"Good evening, Miss Sutherland," he said formally, conscious of the people around them. "Miss Peters."

Molly grinned broadly. "Mr. Hartley! What a surprise to see you here."

"I try to support church functions when I can," Tom replied

"How noble of you," Molly said with a teasing lilt.

"Oh, look! There's Mrs. Wilson. I must speak with her about those curtains she wanted altered." She winked at Annie and slipped away, leaving them alone.

"Subtle, isn't she?" Annie said, watching her friend go.

Tom laughed softly. "About as subtle as a boiler explosion."

"You look tired," Annie said, her voice dropping with concern. "Double shifts again?"

Tom nodded. "And some research after." He glanced around, making sure no one was listening too closely. "I found something. About Drake. I need to tell you, but not here."

Annie's expression grew serious. "Is it about the shop?"

"Partly. It's complicated." Tom ran a hand through his hair. "I didn't mean to bring this up now. Not here."

Annie's gaze softened. "Then don't. For one evening, let's pretend there's no Drake, no debts, no troubles at all."

The music changed, shifting to a lively reel. Couples moved to the center of the room, forming lines for the dance.

Tom hesitated, then extended his hand. "Would

you do me the honor, Miss Sutherland?"

Annie looked at his outstretched hand, then back to his face. "I'm not much of a dancer, Mr. Hartley."

"Neither am I," Tom admitted. "We can be bad at it together."

A smile tugged at the corner of her mouth. "Well, when you put it that way, how can I refuse?"

She placed her hand in his, and Tom felt a jolt at the contact. Her fingers were work-roughened like his own, yet somehow delicate in his grasp. He led her to the dance floor, joining the forming lines.

The music swelled, and the dance began. Tom wasn't skilled, but he knew the basic steps from church socials in his youth. Annie followed his lead, her movements neat and precise, like her stitches in leather.

"You're better at this than you claimed," Tom said as they circled each other.

"So are you," Annie replied. "I expected to be nursing bruised toes by now."

The dance brought them together, then apart, then together again. Each time they touched—hands clasping, arms linking—Tom felt more aware of her, more attuned to the rhythm of her movements.

"Your father didn't come?" he asked during a moment when they stood side by side.

THE COBBLER'S DAUGHTER

Annie shook her head. "He's much improved, but not ready for crowds. Molly's mother is sitting with him."

"She's a good friend."

"The best," Annie agreed. "Though sometimes I could strangle her."

"Like when she abandons you to talk to Mrs. Wilson about curtains?" Tom asked with a smile.

Annie laughed. "Exactly like that."

The dance continued, bringing them back together. This time, when Tom took her hand, he held it a moment longer than necessary.

"We make a good team, Sutherland," he said softly.

Annie's eyes met his, something warm and unguarded in their depths. "Perhaps in some things, Hartley."

The music ended, and the dancers applauded the musicians. Tom reluctantly released Annie's hand but stayed close beside her.

"Would you like some punch?" he asked.

Before Annie could answer, a stir near the entrance caught their attention. The crowd parted slightly, conversation faltering, as Silas Drake entered the hall.

He was immaculately dressed in evening clothes,

his silver-streaked hair combed back from his forehead. On his arm was a younger woman bedecked in jewelry that caught the light from the lanterns.

Reverend Clarke moved immediately to greet them, his expression pleasant but reserved. Drake handed him what appeared to be a sizable donation, making sure those nearby could see the amount.

"What is he doing here?" Annie whispered.

"Making a show," Tom replied, keeping his voice low. "To remind everyone of his position. His power."

Drake's gaze swept the room, acknowledging nods from the town's more prominent citizens. When his eyes fell on Tom and Annie standing together, he paused, his mouth curving in a smile that didn't reach his eyes.

Tom felt Annie tense beside him. He resisted the urge to step in front of her, to shield her from that calculating gaze.

Drake murmured something to the lady, then began making his way across the room toward them. People stepped aside, conversation dimming in his wake.

"Miss Sutherland," Drake said when he reached them. "What a pleasure to see you here. And looking so well."

"Mr. Drake," Annie replied, her voice steady despite the pallor that had crept into her cheeks. "I didn't expect to see you at a church function."

"I support many worthy causes," Drake said smoothly. "The church does such important work for the... less fortunate." His eyes flicked to Tom. "Mr. Hartley, isn't it? From the mill."

"Yes, sir," Tom replied, the words like ashes in his mouth.

"How interesting," Drake said, in the same tone one might use to describe a mildly curious insect. "I understand you've been quite busy lately. Double shifts, visits to the town records office... You're a man of many interests."

"Just trying to improve myself, sir," Tom said, forcing a neutral expression. "A working man should understand the world around him."

Drake's smile thinned. "Indeed. Though some matters are best left to those with the education and position to handle them properly." He turned back to Annie. "Speaking of matters, Miss Sutherland, I believe your next payment is due soon. I trust everything is in order?"

Annie lifted her chin. "We'll meet our obligations, Mr. Drake."

"Excellent." Drake looked between them. "Well, I

won't keep you from your... dancing. Good evening to you both."

He moved away, rejoining his lady among the town's elite on the other side of the room.

Tom felt Annie's hand slip into his, her fingers cold despite the warmth of the hall. He squeezed gently, offering what comfort he could.

"What did you find?" Annie asked. "At the records office."

Tom glanced around. The music had started again, couples moving back to the dance floor. "Not here. Tomorrow, at the shop. I'll come by when I can."

Annie nodded, her eyes still on Drake across the room. "He's planning something. I can feel it."

"So are we," Tom reminded her. "And we have something he doesn't."

"What's that?" Annie asked.

"People who care about more than money." Tom looked around the hall, at the farmers and mill workers, shopkeepers and seamstresses. "People who will stand together when it matters."

Annie followed his gaze, taking in the community gathered around them. "I hope you're right," she said softly. "I really do."

As the social began to wind down, Tom walked

Annie to the church steps. The night air was cool and clear, stars scattered across the sky above them.

"May I walk you home?" Tom asked.

Annie shook her head reluctantly. "Molly is waiting. They're staying with us tonight. Better not to give people more to talk about."

Tom understood. In a small town, reputations were fragile things, especially for a young woman running a business on her own.

"Tomorrow, then," he said. "I'll bring what I found at the records office."

Annie looked up at him, her expression serious in the lamplight. "Be careful, Tom. Drake isn't a man to cross lightly."

"I know." Tom resisted the urge to touch her face, to brush back the strand of hair that had come loose during dancing. "You be careful too. Lock your doors tonight."

Molly appeared at the church door, calling Annie's name. Their moment was over.

"Good night, Tom," Annie said softly.

"Good night, Annie."

He watched her go, joining Molly for the walk back to High Street. Only when they had disappeared from view did Tom turn toward his own lodgings.

ANNIE

Annie sat on the workbench cutting a pattern for a new pair of boots. The shop was quiet, her father still asleep upstairs after working late into the night on a special order. Business had been better since Molly's intervention, with a steady stream of repairs and even a few new orders.

The bell above the door jingled, and Annie looked up to see the postman, a letter in his hand.

"Morning, Miss Sutherland," he said, tipping his hat. "Letter for you. From Drake's office, by the look of it."

Annie set down her knife, wiping her hands on her apron before taking the envelope. "Thank you, Mr. Collins."

"Hope it's nothing troublesome," he said, his expression sympathetic. Everyone in town knew what Drake's letters usually meant.

"I'm sure it's fine," Annie replied with a smile she didn't feel. "Just business."

When the postman left, Annie stared at the envelope, her name and address written in elegant script. The paper was expensive, thick and cream-colored, with "Drake Financial Services" embossed in the corner. She broke the seal and unfolded the letter inside.

The contents were exactly what she'd feared. Due to "market conditions" and "increased risk assessment," the terms of her loan had changed. Her next payment, due in three days, would be double the previous amount. If she couldn't pay, the entire loan would come due immediately.

Annie read the letter twice, her hands beginning to shake. They'd barely managed the regular payments. There was no way they could meet this new demand, not even with the increased business. This wasn't business, it was extortion.

The shop bell jingled again. Annie looked up, expecting another customer, only to freeze at the sight of Silas Drake himself standing in the doorway.

He was impeccably dressed as always, his coat of

fine wool, his boots polished to a mirror shine. A silver-topped cane hung from his arm, though he showed no signs of needing it to walk.

"Miss Sutherland," he said, removing his hat. "I hope I'm not interrupting your work."

Annie quickly folded the letter and tucked it into her pocket. "Mr. Drake. What can I do for you?"

Drake stepped further into the shop, his gaze sweeping over the work area, the boots lined up for repair, the tools hanging on the wall. He touched a piece of leather on the bench, running his fingers over the surface.

"Fine material," he said. "You do quality work here. It's a pity such craftsmanship is becoming a thing of the past."

"Is there something specific you needed, Mr. Drake?" Annie asked, deliberately keeping her voice neutral. "A repair, perhaps?"

Drake smiled, though it didn't reach his eyes. "As a matter of fact, I placed an order for boots some weeks ago. I was passing by and thought I might check on their progress."

Annie frowned. "We have no order under your name, Mr. Drake."

"No? How strange." He tapped his cane against

the floor. "Perhaps it was lost. No matter. I can place one now."

"I'm afraid we're quite busy at the moment," Annie said. "It would be several weeks before we could start a new order."

Drake's smile thinned. "I see. Business has improved, then? How fortunate for you." He moved closer to her workbench. "I noticed you received my letter."

Annie's hand moved instinctively to her pocket. "Yes."

"The terms are quite clear, I trust? Your next payment is due in three days. Double the previous amount."

"Why?" Annie asked, finding her voice. "We've made every payment on time. Why change the terms now?"

Drake gave a casual shrug. "Business, my dear Miss Sutherland. Nothing personal. Markets change, risks increase. It's simply good financial practice to adjust accordingly."

"It's not business," Annie said, unable to keep the anger from her voice. "It's impossible. You know we can't pay that amount."

"Can't you?" Drake's eyebrows rose in mock surprise. "Perhaps you should reconsider some of my previous offers. The factory always needs good hands. The pay is regular, and arrangements could be made regarding your debt."

Annie thought of Marie's injured arm, of the workers pushed to exhaustion, of the "accidents" that seemed to befall those who complained. "No, thank you."

Drake sighed, as if disappointed in a child who refused to see reason. "Then I suppose you'll need to find the money elsewhere. Perhaps your friend Mr. Hartley might help? You two seemed quite close at the church social."

Annie felt her blood run cold. "Mr. Hartley is simply a customer. A neighbor."

"Is he? How interesting." Drake ran his finger along the edge of her workbench. "He's been quite active lately."

He looked up, meeting her eyes. "It would be a shame," he said casually, "if an accident were to happen to such a hardworking young man. The mill can be a dangerous place, after all. Especially the boiler room."

Annie fought to keep her expression neutral, though her heart pounded in her chest.

"Are you threatening Tom?" she asked, her voice steady despite her fear.

Drake looked shocked. "Threatening? My dear Miss Sutherland, I would never threaten anyone. I'm simply expressing concern for a young man who seems to be overextending himself. Working too hard. Taking unnecessary risks."

He picked up his hat, settling it on his head. "I'll expect your payment in three days. The full amount, as specified in the letter. Good day, Miss Sutherland."

The bell jingled as he left, the sound jarring in the quiet shop. Annie stood frozen for a moment, then slowly sank onto her stool. Her hands shook as she pulled the letter from her pocket, reading it again.

The amount was impossible. They didn't have it, couldn't get it in three days. This was Drake's way of forcing them out, of taking the shop for his department store plans.

* * *

THE SEWING SHOP was busy when Annie arrived, women bent over machines or hand-stitching garments at the long tables. The clack of sewing machines and the murmur of voices filled the air, along with the scent of fabric and steam from the pressing area.

Annie spotted Molly near the back, working on what looked like a wedding dress, her needle flashing in and out of white satin. She glanced up as Annie approached, her face brightening.

"Annie! What brings you here midday? Not that I'm not happy to see you."

"I need to talk to you," Annie said quietly. "It's important."

Molly caught her serious tone and nodded. "We're due for a break in ten minutes. Wait for me in the back room? There's tea."

Annie made her way to the small room where the seamstresses took their breaks, a cramped space with a kettle, cups, and a few chairs. To her surprise, several women were already there, gathered around the small table. She recognized Marie, her injured arm still bandaged but looking better than when she'd last seen her. Beside her sat Elizabeth Walsh from the bakery and Sarah Thompson, whose husband ran the general store.

"Annie Sutherland," Elizabeth said with a smile. "Join us. We're just having a quick cup before going back."

Annie took a seat, accepting the cup Marie pushed toward her. "I didn't expect to find so many of you on break at once."

"We take turns," Sariah explained. "Different groups, different times. Keeps the shop running smooth."

The door opened, and Molly slipped in, untying her apron. "I see you've found our little gathering."

"Just happened upon it," Annie said. "I didn't know you all took breaks together."

"Not usually," Marie said, her voice lower than the others. "But lately, we've had reason to."

Something in her tone caught Annie's attention. "What do you mean?"

The women exchanged glances. Then Elizabeth leaned forward. "We've been sharing information. About Drake."

Annie stared at them, surprised. "You have?"

"It started with just me and Marie," Molly explained, sitting beside Annie. "After I heard what happened at his factory. Then Elizabeth joined when Drake's men tried to buy her father's bakery for half its worth."

"And I came in when my husband started receiving threats about our lease," Sariah added. "Drake owns the building now, though we didn't know it when we signed the new agreement."

"There are more of us," Marie said. "Women from

all over town. We meet when we can, share what we know."

Annie looked at each of them in turn, these women she'd known all her life but never truly seen before. They weren't just shopkeepers' wives or factory workers or seamstresses. They were a network, already doing what she and Tom had only just begun.

"I came to talk to Molly about Drake," Annie said slowly. "He visited the shop this morning. After sending a letter demanding double our next loan payment."

"The swine," Elizabeth muttered. "He did the same to my brother last month."

"That's not all," Annie continued. "He threatened Tom. Not directly, but he made it clear Tom could have an 'accident' at the mill if I didn't cooperate."

Molly's eyes widened. "He threatened Tom to your face? That's new. He usually keeps his threats indirect, through his men."

"It means you're getting to him," Marie said, a hint of satisfaction in her voice. "You and Tom both."

"But how?" Annie asked. "We've barely begun gathering information."

"It's not just about information," Sariah said quietly. "It's about resistance. People are starting to talk, to question. The church social was full of whispers, especially after you and Tom danced together. Everyone saw how Drake watched you."

"And you're not the only ones digging," Elizabeth added. "My father's been asking questions at the bank. Sariah 's husband has been tracking which suppliers Drake controls. Little things, but they add up."

Annie felt a flicker of hope. "Have you found anything useful? Anything that could help stop him?"

The women shared another look, then Marie nodded. "We have pieces. Each of us knows something, which buildings he really owns, which businesses he's targeting next, which officials are in his pocket."

"The problem," Molly said, "is putting it all together. We need proof, not just rumors or suspicions."

Annie reached into her pocket and pulled out the letter from Drake. "I have proof of the loan changes. And Tom has documents from the town records office showing property transfers. Mrs. Nazari gave me copies of banking records that show how Drake moves money between businesses."

The women stared at her, then at each other.

"You have actual documents?" Elizabeth asked, her voice hushed.

Annie nodded. "Hidden in the shop. And Drake might be behind the 'accidents' at the mill."

"This could be it," Sarah whispered. "If we combine what you have with what we know..."

"We could build a case against him," Marie finished. "Something no magistrate could ignore, not even Phillips."

Molly's face lit up. "We need to get everyone together. All the women in our network. Share everything we know, everything we have."

"When?" Annie asked. "Where? It would have to be somewhere Drake wouldn't notice."

"The church," Elizabeth suggested. "Wednesday evening during prayer meeting. Most of us attend anyway. Drake never does."

"Perfect," Molly agreed. "We can talk afterward, in the sewing circle room. No one will question women staying to sew and chat."

Annie felt a surge of energy. "I'll bring what I have. But we need to be careful. Drake has eyes everywhere."

"Not everywhere," Marie said with a grim smile. "Men talk in pubs, but women talk everywhere. In kitchens, at market stalls, over laundry lines. Drake watches the men, but he doesn't watch us. Not closely enough."

Annie realized Marie was right. Drake, for all his cunning, had a blind spot. He saw women as either tools to be used or obstacles to be removed, not as threats in their own right. It was a weakness they could exploit.

"I'll be there," Annie promised. "Wednesday evening."

The break time was ending, and they began to gather their cups, preparing to return to work.

As they filed out, Molly hung back with Annie. "Are you all right? Really? Drake threatening Tom..."

Annie shook her head. "I'm worried, Molly. What if Drake does something before we can stop him? What if Tom gets hurt because of me?"

"Tom's a grown man," Molly said gently. "He knows the risks. And he cares for you, Annie. Anyone with eyes can see that."

Annie felt her face warm. "We're friends. Allies."

Molly laughed softly. "Is that what they're calling it these days? I saw you two dancing at the social. That wasn't just friendship."

"Molly!"

"Oh, stop pretending. It's me you're talking to." Molly squeezed her hand. "It's all right to care for someone, Annie. Even in difficult times. Especially in difficult times."

Annie couldn't deny it any longer, not to Molly, not to herself. "I do care for him," she admitted quietly. "More than I should."

"There's no 'should' about it," Molly said firmly. "The heart wants what it wants. And Tom Hartley is a good man. One of the best in this town."

"That's why I can't bear the thought of him being hurt because of me."

"He won't be," Molly assured her. "We won't let that happen. Any of us." She glanced toward the door. "I have to get back. Will you be all right?"

Annie nodded. "I'll see you at church tomorrow. And then Wednesday evening."

"Be careful walking home," Molly cautioned. "Drake might have men watching."

"I will."

* * *

ANNIE SAT beside her father during church service, he insisted on attending despite his lingering weakness. Across the aisle, Tom sat with his mother, their eyes meeting briefly during the opening prayer.

After the service, the congregation spilled out

into the churchyard, people gathering in small groups to chat in the spring sunshine. Annie helped her father down the steps, then saw him settled with Mr. Fletcher and some of the other older men.

She looked around for Tom, finding him near the gate with his mother. Their eyes met again, and this time, Annie made a decision. She walked toward him, her heart beating faster with each step.

"Mrs. Hartley," she said with a smile when she reached them. "How are you today?"

"Quite well, my dear," Sarah Hartley replied, her kind eyes twinkling. "Your father is looking better every week."

"Yes, he's much improved." Annie glanced at Tom, then back to his mother. "I hope you don't mind if I borrow your son for a short walk? There's something I need to discuss with him."

Mrs. Hartley's smile widened. "Not at all. I was just about to join the ladies for tea in the parish hall. You young people enjoy the fine weather."

She patted Tom's arm and moved away, leaving them alone. Tom raised an eyebrow at Annie.

"A walk?" he asked.

Annie nodded. "By the river, if you don't mind. It's... private there."

Tom understood immediately. "Lead the way."

They left the churchyard together, walking side by side down the lane that led to the river path. It was a lovely spring day, warm without being hot, the sky clear blue above them. In the fields beyond the town, wildflowers dotted the green grass with splashes of color.

The river path was quiet, most people still at church or at home preparing Sunday dinner. Annie waited until they were well away from the town before speaking.

"Drake came to the shop yesterday," she said without preamble. "After sending a letter demanding double our next payment."

Tom's expression darkened. "Double? That's impossible. He knows you can't pay that."

"Exactly. That's the point. He wants us to default so he can take the shop." Annie took a deep breath. "But that's not why I wanted to talk to you. He... he mentioned you specifically."

Tom stopped walking, turning to face her. "What did he say?"

Annie met his gaze. "He knows about your visits to the records office. About the meetings with the mill workers. He said it would be a shame if an accident happened to you at the mill. Especially in the boiler room."

She expected Tom to be angry, perhaps even to blame her for putting him in danger. Instead, a slow smile spread across his face.

"What?" Annie asked, confused. "Tom, he threatened you."

"I know," Tom replied. "And it means we're making him nervous. He wouldn't bother threatening us if we weren't getting close to something important."

Annie stared at him. "You're pleased about this?"

"Not pleased, exactly. But it confirms we're on the right track." Tom resumed walking, and Annie fell into step beside him. "We need to move faster... Gather everything we have, present it to someone who can act on it."

"I met with Molly and some other women today," Annie said. "They've been gathering information too, forming a network across town. We're meeting Wednesday evening at the church to share what we know."

Tom looked at her with surprise. "A women's network? How many?"

"Dozens, from what Molly said. Women from the factory, wives of shopkeepers, seamstresses."

Tom let out a low whistle. "That's brilliant. Drake would never suspect."

"That's what Marie said. He watches the men, but he doesn't watch the women." Annie smiled slightly. "His mistake."

They reached a bend in the river where the bank widened into a small, pebbly beach. The water flowed gently here, clear enough to see the stones beneath the surface. Tom stopped, picking up a flat stone.

"Have you ever skipped stones?" he asked, the subject change surprising Annie.

"No," she admitted. "My father tried to teach me once, but I never got the knack of it."

Tom grinned. "It's all in the wrist. Here, let me show you."

He demonstrated, flicking his wrist as he released the stone. It skipped across the water's surface four times before sinking.

"You try," he said, handing her another stone.

Annie took it, attempting to mimic his motion. The stone plopped directly into the water with a disappointing splash.

"Not quite," Tom said, laughing. "Here."

He moved behind her, selecting another stone and placing it in her hand. Then his hand covered hers, his arm guiding hers back.

"Like this," he said, his voice close to her ear. "Pull

back, then forward, with a snap of the wrist at the end."

Together, they threw the stone. It skipped twice before sinking, and Annie let out a delighted laugh.

"Try again on your own."

She did, focusing on the motion he'd shown her. This time, the stone skipped three times. Annie turned to him, smiling widely.

"Did you see that?"

"I did," Tom said, his own smile matching hers. "You're a natural."

For a few minutes, they forgot about Drake. Eventually, they sat on a large rock near the water's edge.

"Did you always want to work at the mill?" Annie asked.

Tom shook his head. "No. I wanted to be a carpenter like my father. I was learning from him, apprenticing. When he died, there wasn't enough work for someone with half-finished training. The mill was hiring, so I went there."

"You could still be a carpenter," Annie said. "Your wood carving is beautiful. I've seen the boxes you made for my father."

Tom looked pleased at her compliment. "Maybe someday. When things are more settled." He skipped another stone. "What about you? Did you always want to be a cobbler?"

Annie thought about it. "I never considered anything else. It was always the shop, always leather and tools and the smell of polish. I can't imagine doing anything different."

"Then we'll make sure you don't have to," Tom said firmly. "Whatever it takes, we'll save your shop."

The simple determination in his voice warmed Annie's heart.

"We should head back," Annie said eventually. "My father will be wondering where I am."

They walked back toward town, neither hurrying. Their hands brushed occasionally, and after the third such touch, Tom's fingers closed gently around hers. Annie felt her heart jump, but she didn't pull away. Instead, she let her fingers intertwine with his, the contact warm and reassuring.

They walked like that, hand in hand, until they reached the edge of town. There, Tom reluctantly released her hand, though they continued to walk close together.

When they reached the cobbler shop, Annie stopped at the door, turning to face Tom.

"Thank you for the walk," she said. "And the stone-skipping lesson."

"My pleasure," Tom replied, his eyes warm as they met hers. "Same time next Sunday?"

Annie nodded. "I'd like that."

Tom raised his hand, hesitated, then gently tucked a strand of hair behind her ear. His fingers lingered for a moment against her cheek, the touch light but sending warmth spreading through her.

"Be careful, Annie," he said softly. "Until Wednesday. Keep your doors locked at night."

"You too," she replied, acutely aware of his closeness, of the concern in his eyes. "No risks at the mill. Promise me."

"I promise."

He stepped back, and Annie felt the loss of his warmth immediately. She knew she was blushing like a schoolgirl, her cheeks hot despite the mild day. Tom smiled, a tender smile that made her heart beat faster.

"Until Wednesday," he said.

"Until Wednesday," she echoed.

ANNIE

Annie's hands trembled slightly as she slipped through the side door of St. Mark's Church Wednesday evening, the heavy wooden panel creaking quietly under her touch. The familiar smell of beeswax candles and aged hymnals greeted her, a small comfort against the churning anxiety in her stomach. She was early, deliberately so, giving herself time to breathe before facing the women who might become allies in her fight against Silas Drake.

The church was dim, illuminated only by a few gas lamps near the altar where Reverend Clarke held midweek prayer meetings. Annie made her way to the small vestry room behind the pulpit, where Molly had arranged for them to gather.

"Annie! You came." Molly's face brightened as she looked up from arranging chairs in a circle. She wore her work dress, the gray fabric speckled with threads from the sewing shop, her hair tied back with a fraying ribbon. "I wasn't certain you would, what with everything at the shop."

"I said I would, didn't I?" Annie replied, removing her thin shawl. "Father's minding the shop. A rare good day for him so he insisted."

"You're the first to arrive. The others should be here soon. Mrs. Thompson is bringing tea."

Annie nodded, helping to arrange the last chair. "How many are coming?"

"Seven, including us. Mrs. Walsh, Marie, Mrs. Thompson, Mrs. Harper from the bakery, and Mrs. Lewis whose husband lost his butcher shop to Drake." Molly paused.

The door opened again, and within minutes, the vestry filled with whispered greetings and the rustle of skirts. These weren't just shopkeepers' wives and workers, they were the backbone of High Street's commerce, women who balanced ledgers and served customers while their husbands received the credit.

Mrs. Thompson arrived with a small kettle and tin cups balanced on a tray, her round face flushed from hurrying. "Had to wait until my husband was occupied with inventory," she explained, pouring steaming tea for each woman.

When all were settled, cups warming hands that spent days sewing, kneading, or counting coins, Molly cleared her throat. "We all know why we're here. Each of us has suffered under Silas Drake's schemes."

Marie nodded, her thin fingers twisting in her lap. "He owns us, some more than others."

"Not for long," Annie said, surprising herself with her firmness. All eyes turned to her, and she sat straighter. "Tom Hartley has been gathering evidence from the mill and getting records showing Drake's manipulation of the wages, unsafe conditions he's ignored, property he's acquired through deception."

"Evidence is well and good," said Mrs. Lewis, a stern woman with graying hair pulled tightly back, "but who would hear it? The magistrate?" She gave a bitter laugh. "My husband approached him when Drake raised the interest on our loan without warning. He dismissed him, said the contract was binding."

Annie nodded. "The magistrate is compromised. Drake paid for Pearson's daughter's wedding. An unusually generous gift between 'mere acquaintances,' as they claim to be."

Mrs. Walsh leaned forward, her worn face lighting with understanding. "So, the courts offer no justice."

"Not the local court," Annie agreed. "But there's the town meeting next week. The county judge, Justice Matthews, always attends. He oversees appeals from our magistrate's decisions."

"And why would this Justice Matthews be different?" asked Mrs. Thompson, skepticism lacing her voice. "Drake's influence reaches far."

Annie set her cup down with a quiet clink. "Because Blackwood has a reputation for fairness, and more importantly, he has no known ties to Drake. He comes from old money and doesn't need Drake's favors. Tom's research hasn't found any connection between them."

"That doesn't mean there isn't one," Mrs. Harper cautioned. "Drake is clever."

"It's a risk," Annie admitted. "But what choice do we have? Drake is strangling this town business by business, person by person. He's raised my interest rate without warning, threatened Tom's safety, and plans to demolish our shops for his department store."

"A department store?" Mrs. Lewis frowned.

Annie quickly shared Mrs. Nazari's information, watching as understanding dawned on each face.

"So that's why he's been buying properties through proxies," Mrs. Walsh said, pulling her shawl tighter. "My landlord sold to a man from Manchester last month and raised the rent the next day."

"He's same man who bought the tannery building," Annie confirmed. "It's all Drake, working through different names."

Molly stood, pacing the small room. "If we combine our evidence with what Tom has gathered, and present it publicly where Drake can't silence us..."

"He'd still deny everything," Mrs. Thompson interrupted. "And who would the town believe? Him, with his fine suits and banking house, or us?"

"Numbers don't lie," Annie said firmly. "And neither do contracts with altered dates and terms. The judge would have to investigate."

A heavy silence fell, broken only by the distant sound of the church clock chiming seven.

"I'll stand with you," Marie said quietly. "I've nothing left to lose. My brother works sixteen hours in Drake's factory to pay a debt that never shrinks."

"I will too," added Mrs. Walsh. "For my son, who Drake had dismissed from the mill when I couldn't pay."

One by one, each woman nodded, some with conviction, others with fear they barely concealed, but all agreed.

"Then we need to organize our evidence and get ready" Annie said,

"We'll need to be careful," Mrs. Lewis warned as they prepared to leave. "Drake has eyes everywhere. If he suspects what we're planning..."

"That's why we meet here, during prayer meeting," Molly said. "Anyone watching would assume we're simply pious women."

Annie slipped her notebook into her pocket. "I'll speak to Tom tomorrow. We'll need to coordinate our evidence."

The women departed in twos and threes, careful not to draw attention. Annie was last to leave with Molly, the two walking briskly through streets growing dark with evening.

"Do you really think the judge will help?" Molly asked as they neared the cobbler shop.

Annie's hand tightened around the notebook in her pocket. "He has to. I don't see another way out."

"It's dangerous, Annie. Drake won't simply accept defeat."

"More dangerous to do nothing," Annie replied, stopping at her shop door. The lamp inside cast a warm glow through the window, showing her father at the workbench. "Either way, we can't continue as we are. Look at what happened to Mrs. Lewis's husband, and to Marie's brother."

Molly squeezed her hand. "Be careful. I'll see you tomorrow."

Annie watched her friend disappear into the twilight before entering the shop, the familiar bell announcing her return. Her father looked up from the boot he was polishing, his face drawn but eyes clear.

"You've been gone a while," he observed. "Prayer meeting must have been spirited tonight."

Annie smiled tiredly. "It was... enlightening." She moved to check the small pot of stew simmering on the back stove, stirring it before ladling portions into two bowls. "You should have eaten without me."

"And miss our only chance to dine together? Not likely." Harold took the bowl she offered, his fingers steadier than they'd been in weeks. "Besides, I had work to finish. Mr. Finch's son brought in his riding boots and paid a fair price too."

They ate at the small table by the shop window, the street outside quiet except for the occasional passerby. Annie watched her father eat with genuine appetite, a welcome change from recent weeks.

"Something's troubling you," Harold said after a while, setting his spoon down. "More than the usual worries."

Annie considered deflecting but found she couldn't. Her father had always been her confidant, even as she tried to shield him from their worst troubles.

"We're planning to confront Drake," she admitted. "At the town meeting next week, when Justice Matthews will be present."

Harold's hand stilled on his cup. "That's a bold move. The town meeting is public, and Drake will be there with his supporters."

"That's why it has to be there. A lot of witnesses will be there. The women I met with tonight, have all suffered under Drake's schemes. Tom has evidence from the mill." She hesitated. "It may be our only chance to stop him from taking the shop."

"And what of the consequences?" her father asked carefully. "Drake isn't known for his forgiveness."

Annie met his gaze. "I know. But what choice do we have? Pay interest that grows faster than we can earn? Or watch him demolish everything for his department store?"

To her surprise, Harold nodded slowly. "Your mother would have done the same," he said quietly. "She always faced troubles head-on, she did."

"You're not angry?"

"Worried, yes. Angry, no." He reached across the table, his calloused hand covering hers. "I'm proud of you, Annie. You've carried this shop, and me, longer than you should have had to. If anyone can stand against Drake and be heard, it's you."

Annie felt her throat tighten. "I'm frightened," she admitted. "Not just of failing, but of what he might do. He's already threatened Tom indirectly."

"The Hartley boy?" Harold's eyebrows rose. "Ah, I see. He matters to you."

"He's risking his position at the mill to help us," Annie replied, feeling her cheeks warm. "All of us, not just me."

Harold smiled slightly. "Of course." He squeezed her hand. "You must be careful, both of you. Drake has built his empire on others' misfortunes. He won't surrender it easily."

"I know," Annie said. "But we have to try."

They finished their meal in thoughtful silence, the weight of the coming confrontation settling between them like an unwelcome guest. When her father retired upstairs, Annie remained at the table, staring at the small notebook bulging with stories of Drake's victims.

It wasn't just about saving their shop anymore. It was about justice for an entire town caught in Drake's web. A town her family had served for generations.

Whatever came at the town meeting, Annie knew there would be no turning back.

TOM

Tom's heart pounded against his ribs as he sat on the hard wooden bench in the town hall one week later. The room was buzzing with talks and filled to capacity with townspeople dressed in their Sunday best. Beside him, Annie sat with her back straight, her green eyes fixed on the raised platform where Justice Edmund Matthews presided. Her hand rested just inches from his on the bench, close enough that he could feel the warmth radiating from her skin.

The justice, a tall man with silver-streaked hair and piercing eyes that seemed to miss nothing, adjusted his spectacles as he surveyed the crowd. He'd been speaking for nearly twenty minutes about county matters, tax collections, and the rule of law.

"And so, we maintain order through proper channels and procedures," Justice Matthews concluded. "Are there any questions before we move to specific petitions?"

Tom felt Annie's subtle glance in his direction. This was the moment they'd planned for. He raised his hand, ignoring the tremor that ran through his tired muscles.

"Yes, the gentleman in the third row," the justice pointed directly at Tom.

Tom stood, aware of the eyes turning toward him. "Thank you, Your Honor. I've a question about justice itself," he said. "What should the people do when they're being oppressed and can't get justice through the usual channels? When those meant to protect them are part of the problem?"

A murmur rippled through the crowd. Justice Matthews' eyebrows rose slightly, but his expression remained measured.

"That is indeed a serious question, young man," he replied. "The law exists to protect all citizens, regardless of their station. If local authorities fail in their duty, there are higher powers to appeal to the county courts, circuit judges, even the Lord Chancellor if necessary. No one should suffer injustice in silence. What is your name, sir?"

"Tom Hartley, Your Honor. I work at Harding's Mill."

"And do you have such a grievance, Mr. Hartley?"

Tom nodded. "I do, Your Honor. As do many others in this town. We have evidence of systematic exploitation and corruption by Mr. Silas Drake."

The crowd murmured. At the front of the hall, Silas Drake rose from his seat, his face darkening with rage.

"This is preposterous!" Drake snapped, turning to face the crowd rather than the justice. "This mill worker knows nothing of business or finance. He's spreading dangerous lies because he's too simple to understand commerce."

Justice Matthews struck his gavel once. "Mr. Drake, you will address the court, not the assembly."

Drake adjusted his posture, smoothing his expensive waistcoat. "My apologies, Your Honor. But this man should be removed for making baseless accusations against a respected businessman."

Two men whom Tom recognized them as part of Drake's circle, moved from their positions near the wall and started toward him. The crowd shifted nervously.

"Stop where you are," the justice commanded. "I haven't authorized anyone's removal." He turned his attention back to Tom. "You claim to have evidence, Mr. Hartley?"

Tom reached inside his jacket and withdrew a folded packet of papers. "Yes, Your Honor. I have property records showing Mr. Drake has secretly acquired businesses through proxies after forcing the original owners into debt. I have ledgers from the mill showing unsafe conditions created to maximize profits at workers' expense."

Drake's face paled slightly. "Your Honor, these are private business matters. They should be discussed in chambers, not aired before a mob."

"They're not private when they affect half the town," Tom countered. "People have lost livelihoods, homes, and some have even lost their lives due to Mr. Drake's schemes."

Justice Matthews held up his hand. "Perhaps Mr. Drake is right about one thing. These are serious allegations that warrant a proper hearing in my chambers…"

"No, Your Honor," Tom interrupted, earning a frown from the justice. "Begging your pardon, but I'm not the only one with something to say. Mr. Drake has harmed many in this room."

The justice studied Tom's face. "Is that so?"

Tom turned to the crowd. "Will those who've suffered at Drake's hands please stand?"

For a terrible moment, nothing happened. Tom felt his heart sink. Then Annie stood beside him, raising her chin proudly. Across the aisle, Billy and his father struggled to their feet. Jack Davidson stood with a groan, followed by Mrs. Wilson, who clutched her walking stick tightly.

Like a slow wave, people began to rise throughout the room. The Fletchers. The Nazari's. Molly Peters and the women from the sewing shop. One by one, nearly half the assembly was standing.

Justice Matthews' eyes widened as he surveyed the room. "This is... most unusual."

"It's a conspiracy, Your Honor!" Drake protested, his composure cracking. "This mill worker has organized a mob to attack my reputation. I demand protection!"

"It's no conspiracy," came a voice from the crowd. Tom turned to see Mr. Jenkins, the mill clerk, standing with a leather-bound ledger in his hands. "I've kept records of Mr. Drake's dealings with Mr. Harding. How they arranged 'accidents' to fire workers without compensation and how they've been skimming wages."

Mr. Nazari stepped forward next. "He's been

buying properties through false names, Your Honor. I have the documents here proving he plans to demolish our shops for his own gain."

"And he charges interest rates that make repayment impossible," added Frank Wiley, waving a loan agreement. "Twenty percent a month compounded. No honest man could design such terms."

Silas Drake's face had turned ashen. "These are business matters, Your Honor. Perhaps I've been firm, but nothing illegal..."

"The law's clear on usury, Mr. Drake," Justice Matthews cut him off. "And those interest rates, if accurate, far exceed legal limits."

Annie stepped forward, her voice clear and strong. "Your Honor, Mr. Drake threatened physical harm to Tom when I couldn't meet his suddenly doubled payment demands. He told me explicitly that if I didn't pay, Tom would have an 'accident' at the mill."

A shocked silence fell over the room. Justice Matthews' expression hardened as he looked at Drake.

"That, sir, would constitute criminal intimidation, a most serious offense."

Drake looked around wildly. "She's lying! They're all lying!" His eyes darted toward the door. "This is absurd. I won't stand here and be slandered by the rabble."

As Drake took a step toward the exit, Justice Matthews's voice rang out. "Mr. Drake, you will remain exactly where you are. Constable Adams, please ensure Mr. Drake stays with us while we sort this matter."

The town constable, who had been sitting near the back, moved quickly to block the door.

"Your Honor," Tom said, stepping forward with his packet of evidence, "we've gathered testimonies, records, loan agreements, property documents, and mill logs. Everything is organized and ready for your review."

Justice Matthews nodded slowly. "I see this will require more than a passing examination." He addressed the crowd. "This hearing will be suspended for one hour while I review these materials in my temporary chambers. Mr. Drake will remain in the custody of Constable Adams. Those with evidence to present, please organize yourselves with Mr. Hartley's assistance."

* * *

Tom stood shifting his weight from one foot to another as the crowd whispered with speculation. The hour Justice Matthews had taken to review the evidence felt like three. He caught Annie's eye across the aisle where she sat with her father, and she gave him a small, tight smile that didn't reach her eyes. Her hands were clasped so tightly in her lap that her knuckles had gone white.

The side door opened, and Justice Matthews strode in, his face grave as he took his place at the front of the hall. The room fell silent immediately.

"After reviewing the substantial evidence provided," the justice began, "I find there are serious allegations of misconduct that warrant immediate action."

Tom felt his heartbeat quicken. This was the moment that would decide whether their weeks of risk and planning had been worth it.

Justice Matthews adjusted his spectacles and continued. "I hereby issue an immediate suspension of all of Mr. Drake's financial operations pending a full investigation. All loan agreements are frozen at their current principal amounts, with no further interest to be accrued or payments to be collected."

A collective gasp went through the room. Tom stared, hardly believing what he was hearing.

"Furthermore, I am ordering a full court hearing

to be convened in three weeks' time at the county courthouse, where these allegations will be heard in detail. Mr. Drake will present himself at that time to answer these charges formally."

Drake shot to his feet. "This is outrageous! You cannot..."

"I can and I have, sir," the justice cut him off sharply. "And I would advise you to secure competent legal representation rather than continuing to interrupt these proceedings."

Drake subsided, his face a mask of barely contained fury.

Justice Matthews wasn't finished. "I must also censure Magistrate Phillips for his apparent complicity in these matters. The evidence suggests he has repeatedly ignored valid complaints and favored Mr. Drake's interests over proper application of the law."

Tom's eyes found Magistrate Phillips, who seemed to shrink in his chair near the front of the room.

"Magistrate Phillips is hereby removed from his position, effective immediately. I will recommend to the Lord Chancellor that a replacement be appointed forthwith." Justice Matthews struck his gavel with finality. "This hearing is adjourned. I will remain in town for the next several days to oversee the settlement of accounts and ensure an orderly transition."

The hall erupted in a mixture of cheers, shocked exclamations, and fervent discussion. Tom watched as Drake rose from his seat, his face twisted with rage. The businessman straightened his jacket with sharp, angry movements and strode toward the exit, flanked by his two men.

The crowd parted for him, but not with the deference he was accustomed to. Several people jeered as he passed. Mrs. Wilson pointedly turned her back on him. Jack Davidson spat on the floor near Drake's polished boots. The man who had held the town in his grip for years was walking out with his authority in tatters, and everyone knew it.

Tom made his way through the crowd toward Annie, accepting handshakes and shoulder claps from people he barely knew. He saw Molly rush to Annie from the other side of the room, throwing her arms around her friend in an exuberant embrace. Annie's face broke into the first genuine smile he'd seen from her in weeks.

"We did it," Jack Davidson said, appearing at Tom's elbow. "Never thought I'd see the day."

"We did," Tom agreed, still struggling to believe it himself. "Though there's still the hearing to come."

"Aye, but he's finished in this town regardless," Jack said, his weathered face creased in a rare smile. "No one will fear him now they've seen him cut down to size."

Tom nodded, his eyes still on Annie. "Excuse me, Jack. There's someone I need to speak with."

He made his way to where Annie stood with Molly and her father. Harold Sutherland looked years younger, the worried lines on his face softened with relief.

"Mr. Hartley," Harold greeted him, extending his hand. "It seems we owe you a considerable debt of gratitude."

Tom shook the older man's hand. "It was all of us together, sir. Your daughter was just as crucial to our success, perhaps more so."

Annie's cheeks colored slightly, but she held his gaze. "It was indeed a group effort. I don't think any of us could have managed alone."

"Even so," Harold said, "I believe I'll go thank the justice personally. Molly, would you accompany an old man? I find I'm a bit unsteady after all the excitement."

Tom noticed the meaningful look Harold gave

his daughter before offering his arm to a beaming Molly. It was about as subtle as a factory whistle, but Tom wasn't going to complain.

"Would you allow me to walk you home?" Tom asked when they had gone. "It's getting late, and you must be tired."

"I'd like that," Annie replied. "Though I'm not sure I could sleep now if I tried. I feel as though I've had ten cups of strong tea."

They left the hall together, stepping out into the cool air. The street was busy with people from the meeting, gathered in small groups, talking excitedly about what had happened. Several nodded or tipped their hats to Tom and Annie as they passed.

"I keep expecting to wake up and find this was all a dream," Annie said as they turned onto High Street. "Did you see Drake's face when the justice suspended his operations?"

"I did," Tom replied, unable to suppress a smile. "I suspect that's the first time in years anyone's told him no and made it stick."

"And Magistrate Phillips! I never expected the justice to remove him on the spot like that."

"That was Justice Matthews' cleverest move," Tom observed. "Drake's been hiding behind Phillips' authority for years. With Phillips gone, half his protection vanishes."

They walked in silence for a few moments. The air was sweet with the scent of spring blossoms from the gardens they passed.

"What will you do now?" Annie asked. "Will you stay at the mill?"

Tom considered the question. "For now, yes. Someone needs to make sure Harding doesn't try to carry on Drake's practices. And with the justice staying to help settle accounts, there might be a chance to improve conditions properly."

"You could end up as foreman, you know," Annie said. "You understand the work better than most, and the men respect you."

"Perhaps," Tom acknowledged, surprised by the thought. "And what about you? Will you continue with the shop now that Drake's hold is broken?"

Annie nodded firmly. "Father's already talking about new designs. And with our debts frozen and possibly reduced after the hearing, we might actually have a chance to compete properly with those factory boots."

They reached the cobbler shop, its simple sign swinging slightly in the evening breeze. The upper windows glowed with lamplight, Harold had obviously hurried home through a back route to give them privacy, a realization that made Tom both grateful and nervous.

"Annie," he said, turning to face her before she could reach for the door. "I've been wanting to ask you something, but I thought it best to wait until this business with Drake was settled."

She looked up at him. "Yes?"

Tom suddenly found his carefully prepared words had deserted him. "I was wondering if you might... that is, if you would consider..."

"Yes?" she prompted again, a small smile playing at the corners of her mouth.

He took a deep breath. "Would you allow me to call on you properly? Not to discuss Drake or loans or mill conditions, but simply to enjoy your company?"

The smile bloomed fully on her face. "I would like that very much, Tom."

"You would?" He couldn't quite keep the surprise from his voice.

"Did you think I'd say no?" she asked, her eyes twinkling with amusement.

"I thought you might have more important things to attend to now that the shop has a chance to thrive again."

"There will always be boots to mend and leather to cut," she said. "But I've learned these past weeks that there are some things more important than work."

Relief and joy swept through Tom. On impulse, he leaned forward and pressed a quick, soft kiss to her cheek.

"Thank you," he said, stepping back immediately, worried he'd been too forward.

But Annie didn't look offended. If anything, her smile had grown warmer. "Sunday afternoon," she said. "Father will be visiting the Fletchers. Perhaps you could come by then?"

"I'll be here," Tom promised.

ANNIE

Annie's fingers were stiff from hours of work, but she pressed on. The shop was silent except for the occasional crackle from the small stove in the corner and the steady rhythm of her awl puncturing leather.

"Just two more," she murmured to herself, easing another stitch through the tough sole of a work boot.

Three days had passed since the town meeting that had exposed Silas Drake's schemes. Three days of cautious optimism as Justice Matthews's investigation began. Three days of increased business as townspeople, emboldened by recent events, brought repairs they'd been putting off.

She should be upstairs, she thought, glancing

toward the ceiling where her father slept. The hour was indecently late, but she'd promised these boots by morning. The extra coin would help rebuild their savings, now that Drake's crushing debt had been suspended pending the investigation.

A smile tugged at her lips as she recalled Tom's face when Justice Matthews had declared the investigation open. His eyes had found hers across the crowded hall, relief and something warmer passing between them. Sunday. He'd be calling on Sunday.

The shop bell jangled harshly, startling her from her thoughts. Annie frowned, setting down her work. Who would come at this hour? The local drunkards were still at the Fox and Hound, and decent folk were abed.

"We're closed," she called, rising from her stool. "Return in the morning."

Instead of retreating footsteps, the door crashed fully open. Three men pushed inside, their faces shadowed by caps pulled low. The first was tall and broad-shouldered with a scar running through his lip. The second was wiry and quick-moving and the third remained by the door, keeping watch.

"What do you..." Annie began, but the words died in her throat as the scarred one advanced.

"Miss Sutherland," he said, voice like gravel. "You're needed elsewhere."

Annie backed up against her workbench, her heart thundering against her ribs. "Get out of my shop," she demanded, gripping her awl tightly.

The wiry one laughed. "Hear that, Burke? The little cobbler's giving orders."

"I said get out!" Annie brandished the awl and waved the steel point in the air.

Burke lunged forward, faster than his bulk suggested, and knocked the tool from her hand. It clattered across the floorboards as his fingers clamped around her wrist.

"No choice in the matter, miss," he growled, yanking her forward.

Annie twisted violently, kicking at his shins. "Let go of me!" Her free hand found a hammer on the bench behind her. She swung it with all her strength, connecting with his shoulder.

He cursed, grip loosening just enough for her to wrench free. She darted toward the stairs, screaming, "Father! Help!"

The wiry man intercepted her, throwing her against the counter. Pain flared in her hip as it struck the hard edge.

"Shut her up, Finch!" Burke hissed.

She heard footsteps on the stairs. It was her father, awakened by her cries.

"Annie?" Harold's voice was thick with sleep and confusion. He appeared at the bottom of the stairs, grayer and thinner than ever in his nightshirt. "What's happening? Who are you men?"

"Father, run!" Annie shouted, struggling against Finch's hold.

Harold took a step forward, pointing his walking stick to the man. "Unhand my daughter immediately!"

Burke moved toward him with lazy confidence. "Stay out of this, old man."

"I'll summon the constable," Harold threatened.

Annie saw Burke's arm move and he brutally shoved her father backward. Harold's cane clattered away as he fell, landing heavily on the wooden floor with a sickening thud and a cry of pain.

"Father!" Annie screamed. She stomped hard on Finch's foot and twisted free, rushing toward Harold's crumpled form.

Burke caught her around the waist, lifting her bodily from the ground as she kicked and clawed.

"Leave him alone!" she cried. "He's ill, you could kill him!"

Harold struggled to rise, face contorted with

pain. "Annie..."

"Bring her," Burke ordered Finch. "And gag her before she wakes the whole street."

A rag was forced between Annie's teeth, it tasted of coal dust and sweat, and it made her gag. She fought with every ounce of strength, her eyes fixed on her father as they dragged her toward the door.

The last glimpse she had was of Harold reaching a trembling hand toward her, his face ashen in the dim light.

Then they were outside in the cold night air. A wagon was waiting with a fourth man at the reins. Burke lifted her like a sack of flour and tossed her into the back, where some rough hands bound her wrists with coarse rope. A canvas was thrown over her, plunging her into darkness as the wagon lurched into motion.

Annie lay stunned, every jolt of the wheels sent shockwaves through her bruised body. Fear for her father overwhelmed her. Had they killed him? Would anyone find him before morning?

She tried to focus, to note the turns they made, but soon, she lost track in the smothering darkness. The journey lasted perhaps twenty minutes before the wagon stopped. The canvas was ripped away, and Annie was hauled upright.

They were outside a warehouse near the river docks. The windows were boarded, the brick façade crumbling at the edges. It had once been a wool depot, she thought distantly, abandoned after the fire three years past.

Burke dragged her inside, past empty loading bays and into a vast space that smelled of damp and rot. A single lantern cast long shadows across debris-strewn floors. They forced her onto a wooden crate, retying her hands behind her back.

"Comfortable, Miss Sutherland?" Burke asked, removing her gag.

Annie spat at his feet. "My father… if he's harmed..."

"You should worry about yourself," Finch sneered, lighting another lantern.

"Why have you brought me here?" she demanded.

Burke shrugged. "Just following orders. Sit tight."

They retreated to a corner, leaving Annie alone with her thoughts. She tested her bonds, but they held tight, the rope cutting into her wrists whenever she strained against it. Her mouth was dry with fear, but she refused to show it, sitting as straight as her bound arms allowed.

Tom will realize something's wrong when I don't

meet him Sunday, she thought. But Sunday was three days away.

Minutes stretched into what felt like hours. The warehouse creaked and settled around her. Somewhere, water dripped in one drop per second. Her arms ached, and her hip throbbed where she'd struck the counter.

She heard the sound of carriage wheels outside, followed by footsteps. Annie's heart stuttered as a familiar silhouette appeared in the doorway.

Silas Drake stepped into the lantern light, immaculate despite the late hour in his tailored coat and gleaming boots. He carried a walking stick with a silver handle that caught the dim light as he approached.

"Miss Sutherland," he said, as if they were meeting at a social gathering. "I apologize for the unceremonious invitation."

Annie met his gaze without flinching. "Is this how you conduct all your business, Mr. Drake? Through kidnapping and assault?"

He smiled thinly. "Only when conventional methods prove... ineffective." He gestured to Burke, who pulled over another crate for Drake to perch upon, facing Annie. "You've caused me considerable inconvenience."

"Justice Matthews seems to think you've caused this town considerable harm," she countered.

Drake's eyes hardened, though his smile remained fixed. "Justice Matthews will be returning to the county seat shortly, leaving this unfortunate misunderstanding behind him."

"Misunderstanding?" Annie scoffed. "We presented evidence of systematic fraud, intimidation, and exploitation. That's hardly a misunderstanding."

"Evidence can be discredited," Drake said coolly. "Witnesses can recant. Memories become... unreliable."

Annie's mouth went dry. "Is that why I'm here? To be threatened into silence?"

Drake twirled his walking stick idly. "You're here because you've become the rallying point for this tedious rebellion. You and that mill worker, Hartley."

At Tom's name, Annie's chest tightened with fear far greater than what she felt for herself. "Leave him out of this."

"I'm afraid that's impossible. He's made himself quite central to these... accusations." Drake leaned forward. "But you could help him avoid the consequences of his misguided crusade."

"What do you want?" Annie asked, her voice barely above a whisper.

"Control your dogs, Miss Sutherland," Drake said flatly. "Hartley and the others. Tell them to retract their statements. Explain that your emotions ran high, and the facts were misconstrued. Justice Matthews will be persuaded."

Annie stared at him in disbelief. "And if I refuse?"

"Then Hartley loses more than his position at the mill. The boarding house where he lives might suddenly become... uninhabitable. His ailing mother could find herself without a roof." Drake's voice remained conversational. "As for you and your father… well, the shop is still heavily in debt. I could call in that loan immediately."

"You can't," Annie said. "Justice Matthews suspended..."

"Temporarily," Drake cut in. "And paper trails can be adjusted to show the debt predates any alleged impropriety." His gaze bore into hers. "Your father looked quite frail tonight. I wonder how he'd fare in debtors' prison?"

White-hot anger surged through Annie, burning away her fear. "You won't get away with this. The whole town knows what you've done."

"The town will forget," Drake said dismissively.

"They always do. When offered the choice between comfortable ignorance and uncomfortable truth, most choose the former." He stood, looming over her. "So, what will it be, Miss Sutherland? Will you be reasonable?"

Annie lifted her chin, meeting his cold gaze. "I'd rather see my shop burned to the ground than help you continue to prey on innocent people."

Something dangerous flashed in Drake's eyes. "Perhaps you misunderstand your position. You are not negotiating; you are being informed of what will happen."

"And you misunderstand mine," Annie shot back. "I won't be bullied or bribed into betraying this town or Tom Hartley."

Drake's hand moved suddenly, striking her cheek with enough force to snap her head to the side. Pain bloomed hot and sharp in her face, bringing involuntary tears to her eyes.

"Your father raised a fool," he hissed, all pretense of civility gone. "Perhaps a night in this place will help you reconsider your loyalty to a man who won't even be able to protect you."

Annie tasted blood where her teeth had cut the inside of her cheek, but she met his gaze steadily. "Better a fool than a coward who preys on the weak."

Drake's face contorted with fury. He gripped his walking stick so tightly that for a moment, Annie thought he might strike her with it, but he mastered himself with visible effort.

"You will pay for this defiance," he said, his voice cold and precise. "And not just with money. By the time I'm finished, you'll wish you'd accepted my generous offer."

He turned sharply and strode toward the door, pausing to address Burke. "Keep her secure. No food, no water. I'll return in the morning to see if a night's reflection has improved her attitude." His gaze slid to Annie one last time. "Though I doubt it will improve her prospects."

The door slammed behind him, leaving Annie alone with her captors, her cheek stinging and the metallic taste of blood in her mouth.

Don't cry, she told herself fiercely. Don't give them the satisfaction.

Instead, she began to mentally catalog everything around her like the layout of the warehouse, the number of men, those patrolling. If an opportunity came, she would be ready. And if it didn't...

Tom would come looking. Or Molly. Someone would notice her absence. All she had to do was endure until then.

TOM

⚜

Tom's heart raced ahead of his feet as he hurried down High Street toward Sutherland's Cobbler Shop. The sun had barely crested the rooftops, painting the cobblestones with golden light that belied the uneasiness in his gut. No matter how exhausted he'd been from his double shift, he'd barely slept, his thoughts circling around Annie like moths to a flame.

He smoothed down his freshly pressed shirt, purchased with a bit of his savings. Not that Annie seemed to care about such things, but he wanted to look his best when he asked if he could properly court her. He was coming a few days earlier than Sunday, but he needed to do this now.

The shop came into view, and Tom frowned. The

door stood slightly ajar, unusual for the meticulous Sutherlands. A cold feeling settled in his stomach.

"Annie?" he called, pushing the door open wider. The bell gave a discordant jingle.

The shop was silent. No sound of leather being worked, no soft humming that often-accompanied Annie's stitching. Just... nothing.

Then he heard a weak groan from behind the counter.

"Mr. Sutherland?" Tom jumped over the counter, landing hard on his knees beside Harold's crumpled form. The older man's face was ashen, a dark bruise blooming along his temple, dried blood crusted at his hairline.

"Tom," Harold wheezed, fingers clutching weakly at Tom's sleeve. "They took her. They took my Annie."

Tom's blood turned to ice. "Who took her? When?" He helped Harold to sit against the counter, scanning the shop for signs of struggle. An overturned stool. A leather punch on the floor. The faint scuff marks of multiple boot heels.

"Drake's men." Harold's voice cracked. "Last night. Three of them. Burke and Finch... don't know the other. I tried to stop them." His face crumpled. "I couldn't protect her."

Tom's hands clenched into fists. "This isn't your fault." The rage building inside him was so intense it nearly choked him. "I'm getting help. We'll find her."

He helped Harold to a chair, poured him water from the pitcher on the workbench, and pressed it into his trembling hands. "Drink this. Don't try to move. I'll be back with help."

Tom burst out of the shop and sprinted down the street. Jack Davidson lived just two streets over. Ned Porter was likely at the mill by now. Billy was too young for this. Robert Burns would be at the ironworks. In ten minutes, Tom had rounded up six men, breathlessly explaining the situation as they gathered in front of the cobbler shop.

"Drake's gone too far this time," Jack said, "Taking a woman from her home is beyond the pale."

Davidson nodded. "Justice Matthews would have his hide for this alone."

"We need to find her first," Tom said. "Before Drake does something worse."

Back inside, Harold had managed to clean his face. His eyes were clearer now, burning with a father's fury and fear. "They came through the main door. Annie was working late. I heard the commotion and came down, but they were already dragging her out."

"Did they say where they were taking her?" Tom asked.

Harold shook his head. "Just that Drake wanted to 'have a word with her.' The big one, Burke, hit me when I tried to stop them. Next thing I knew, you were here."

Tom nodded. "Davidson, fetch Doctor Perkins for Mr. Sutherland. Robert, check the docks. Drake owns warehouses there. Jack, with me. We'll start asking questions. The rest of you please spread out. Someone must have seen something."

The men dispersed like a well-oiled machine. Tom and Jack headed to the Fox and Hound first, the barkeep, Willis, knew everything that happened after dark.

"Three men with a struggling woman?" Willis scratched his chin. "Can't say I saw that myself, but Maisie's boy was out late collecting night soil. He said something about seeing men carrying something down toward the river warehouses. Thought it was smugglers with goods."

Tom exchanged a look with Jack. The river warehouses had three abandoned buildings that Drake had acquired last year, supposedly for expansion.

They were halfway there when they encountered Mrs. Wilson, wringing her hands in the street.

"Tom Hartley! I was just coming to find help. I couldn't sleep last night because of my hip, you know but I saw from my window. Those terrible men from Drake's office. They had a poor young lady, down River Street. She all wrapped up in something. I should have raised the alarm then, but they looked so dangerous..."

"Which warehouse, Mrs. Wilson?" Tom asked, his voice tight.

"The old coop's building, I think. The one with the blue door, all peeling now."

Tom knew it. The largest of the three, furthest from town. And very isolated.

"Jack, gather the others. Meet me there. And bring whatever tools you can find." Tom was already moving, his walk turning into a run.

"You can't go alone, lad," Jack called after him.

"I'm not waiting."

He approached the warehouse from the river side, crouching low among the tall reeds. The building loomed gray and oppressive against the morning sky, its windows boarded up, the blue door Mrs. Wilson mentioned hanging askew on rusted hinges.

Two men lounged outside the door, smoking. Finch, Tom recognized, his lean frame unmistakable.

The other must be the third man Harold hadn't known. He was taller than Finch but not as massive as Burke would be.

Tom circled the building, finding a broken window at the back. Carefully, he pulled himself up and through, dropping silently onto a dusty floor inside. The warehouse was cavernous, filled with abandoned barrels and crates. He crept forward, guided by the sound of voices.

"...should've been back by now," a gruff voice was saying. Must be Burke, Tom guessed.

"Drake said he had business to attend to first." That was Finch's nasal whine. "We're to keep her quiet until he returns."

Tom peered around a stack of crates. Annie sat tied to a chair in the center of the open space, her head bowed, hair falling loose around her face. Even from this distance, Tom could see the dark mark on her cheek. A bruise. Rage surged through him before he tamped it down. Not yet.

"She's barely said a word since we brought her in," Burke complained. "Drake won't be happy if she's not more cooperative when he returns."

Tom withdrew, circling back to find anything he could use as a weapon. He found a rusty but solid iron bar among the debris and tested its weight in his hand. Not ideal, but it would have to do.

A commotion outside saved him from having to form a more elaborate plan. Jack had arrived with the others, creating a distraction at the front. Tom heard Finch and the third man move toward the door, leaving only Burke with Annie.

Tom didn't hesitate. He rushed from behind the crates, iron bar raised. Burke turned, surprise widening his eyes for only a second before Tom brought the bar down hard against his outstretched arm. There was a sickening crack, and Burke howled.

"Tom!" Annie's head jerked up, her voice hoarse but strong.

Burke lunged despite his broken arm, but Tom was quicker, fueled by a protective fury he'd never felt before. He ducked the wild swing and drove his fist into Burke's stomach, following with a blow to the jaw that sent the larger man staggering.

"Annie, are you hurt?" Tom asked, keeping his eyes on Burke as he circled toward her.

"I'm alright," she said, though the tremor in her voice suggested otherwise. "My father..."

"He's safe. Doctor Perkins is with him." Tom

reached her, quickly working at the ropes binding her wrists. "We've come to take you home."

The front door burst open, and Jack led the charge inside, accompanied by Robert, Davidson, and several other men from town. Outnumbered, Finch and the third man backed away, though Finch reached for something in his coat.

"I wouldn't," Jack said, displaying the heavy wrench in his hand with meaning.

Voices rose outside with more townspeople arriving, drawn by the commotion or summoned by Jack's network.

Then the back door opened, and Silas Drake himself stepped in, freezing at the scene before him. His cold eyes darted from his fallen men to Annie, now free and standing beside Tom, to the gathering crowd at the front.

"This is a private matter," Drake said, with the authority of a man used to being obeyed. "These people are trespassing on my property."

"Kidnapping a woman is a hanging offense," Tom replied, his arm protectively around Annie's shoulders. "As is assault."

Drake's face hardened, but Tom could see him counting odds his odds and weighing risks. With a subtle nod, he began backing toward the door he'd entered through.

"This isn't over, Hartley," he spat. "The girl signed a contract. She owes me."

"Any contract signed under duress is invalid," came a new voice. Reverend Clarke stepped through the crowd, his normally gentle face stern. "Justice Matthews confirmed as much when I wired him this morning. Your operations are suspended, Mr. Drake, pending investigation. I suggest you leave town while you still can."

Drake's face twisted with rage, but he was smart enough to recognize defeat when it stared him in the face. Without another word, he turned and slipped out the door.

"After him!" someone shouted, and a portion of the crowd followed.

"Let him go," Tom said, but they weren't listening to him anymore. The dam had broken on years of fear and resentment. As Drake fled down the riverbank, the crowd followed, their shouts echoing in the morning air.

"Thief!"

"Extortionist!"

"Get out of our town!"

Tom turned to Annie, his concern only for her

now. Her face was pale beneath the bruise on her cheek, her eyes too bright. "Can you walk? We should get you to your father."

Annie nodded, then surprising him, stepped forward and wrapped her arms tightly around his waist, pressing her face against his chest. Tom held her, one hand cradling the back of her head, the other secure around her waist, as if he could shield her from all the harm in the world.

"I knew you'd come," she whispered against his shirt. "I told Drake you would."

Tom's throat tightened. "I'll always come for you, Annie Sutherland."

For a long moment, they stood like that, holding each other while the sounds of the crowd pursuing Drake faded into the distance. Around them, the other men tactfully busied themselves securing Burke and the others.

"Let's go home," Tom said finally, reluctantly loosening his embrace but keeping one arm firmly around her waist.

Annie looked up at him, her green eyes steady despite everything she'd endured. "Yes," she said simply. "Home."

ANNIE

~~~~

Annie stared at the letter in her hand for the fifth time, tracing the official seal from the magistrate's court. The words hadn't changed since the first reading, but they still seemed unbelievable, like raindrops falling upward or the sun rising in the west.

"All loans issued by Silas Drake Financial Services to Annie Elizabeth Sutherland have been declared null and void due to evidence of fraudulent practices..."

She dropped into her workbench chair, legs suddenly unreliable. Two weeks of anxious waiting since Drake had been hauled off by the townspeople, and now freedom was delivered in black ink on cream paper.

"Good news then?" Harold called from where he was polishing a gentleman's boot, his voice stronger than it had been in months. The new medicine had worked wonders, and standing up to Drake seemed to have revived something in him that had been dormant for too long.

Annie tried to answer but found her throat had closed up. Instead, she crossed the shop floor and handed him the letter, watching his eyes widen as he scanned the document.

"We're free of him," she finally managed.

Harold lowered the letter, his gaze finding hers. "Not just free of the debt, Annie. Free of the fear." He reached out and squeezed her hand. "I've never been more proud of you."

The shop bell jangled, and Annie quickly wiped at her eyes before she turned. It slipped immediately when she saw Tom Hartley standing in the doorway, looking unfairly handsome in clean trousers and a pressed shirt, his usual coal dust and mill grime notably absent.

"Bad time?" he asked, taking in their faces with concern.

"Quite the opposite," Harold answered, waving the letter. "Court's ruled Drake's loans invalid."

Tom's face split into a wide grin that made something twist pleasantly in Annie's chest. "That's brilliant news!" He crossed to Harold, clapping him on the shoulder before turning to Annie. "I knew Justice Matthews would come through."

"Did you now?" she asked, finding her voice again. "You seemed considerably less confident when you were pacing outside the courthouse last Tuesday."

"That wasn't lack of confidence," Tom protested. "That was... strategic concern."

Harold chuckled. "I'll leave you two to debate the semantics." He folded the letter carefully, like a treasure map, and tucked it into his waistcoat pocket. "I've a pattern to finish upstairs."

As her father disappeared into their living quarters, Annie became acutely aware of how alone they were. Since the night of her rescue from Drake's warehouse, Tom had visited daily, ostensibly to check on her recovery, though they both knew it had become about more than that. Her bruises had faded, but something else had bloomed in their place.

"You're not working at the mill today?" she asked, busying herself with organizing leather scraps that were already perfectly arranged.

"Finished my shift early. Seems the new mill

ownership has some radical ideas about not working men to death." His tone was light, but they both knew how close he'd come to collapse working those double shifts.

After Drake's arrest, a consortium of local businessmen had purchased the mill, with Reverend Clarke heading the board of trustees. The first order of business had been eliminating the brutal night shifts and raising wages to a living standard.

"Anyway," Tom continued, suddenly looking less sure of himself, "I wondered if you might fancy a walk this evening? The weather's fine, and there's something I'd like to show you."

Annie glanced at the half-repaired boots on her bench, then back at Tom's hopeful face. "I don't mind."

"Excellent!" The relief in his voice was almost comical. "I'll come by around seven? After you've closed up shop?"

She nodded, ignoring the flutter in her stomach. "Seven it is."

When he'd gone, Annie pressed her hands to her heated cheeks. It wasn't as though they hadn't spent time together since that night. They'd given statements to Justice Matthews side by side. They'd attended church together with her father and his mother. They'd even shared tea in this very shop numerous times.

But this felt different. This felt like... Courting.

Annie spent the remainder of the afternoon stitching but she kept pricking her finger twice in the process. By six-thirty, she'd swept the shop floor three times and changed her blouse twice, finally settling on the blue one that brought out her eyes, according to Molly, who had an opinion on everything sartorial.

Her father watched her fluttering about with poorly concealed amusement.

"You could just admit you've taken a shine to the boy," he said mildly.

"I've done nothing of the sort," she replied, too quickly. "Tom's been a good friend to us."

"Indeed." Harold nodded solemnly. "That's why you're wearing your mother's locket and have changed your hair three times."

Annie touched the silver locket at her throat. "I just thought... since we received good news..."

Harold's expression softened. "She would have liked him very much, Annie. Almost as much as I do."

The shop bell saved her from having to respond, and there was Tom, seven on the dot, looking nervous and excited all at once.

"Ready?" he asked.

Annie nodded, retrieving her shawl. "Don't wait up," she told her father, who was suddenly very absorbed in a catalog of leather goods.

"Wouldn't dream of it," Harold replied innocently.

Outside, the evening air was cool but not cold, the last of the day's warmth lingering in the cobblestones beneath their feet. They walked for a few minutes, leaving the bustle of High Street behind.

"Where are we going?" Annie finally asked as they turned toward the river path.

"You'll see." Tom's smile was mysterious, but the hand he offered her was steady. "Trust me?"

She placed her palm against his, their fingers interlocking as naturally as if they'd been doing it for years. "Against my better judgment."

The river path wound through a stand of willows before opening onto a small clearing. Annie gasped softly at the sight before her. A blanket had been laid on the grassy bank, flanked by two lanterns casting a warm glow. A basket sat in the center alongside a small vase of wildflowers.

"Tom," she breathed. "What is all this?"

He rubbed the back of his neck, a gesture she'd come to recognize meant he was nervous. "I thought we might have a proper celebration. Of the court ruling and... everything else."

"Everything else?" she echoed, her heart suddenly hammering against her ribs.

"The mill improvements, your father's health, Drake being gone..." He paused, looking down at their still-joined hands. "Us."

Annie could have responded with deflection or denial. It would have been safer, certainly. But looking at him in the golden lantern light, she found she didn't want safe anymore.

"Us," she agreed softly.

They settled on the blanket, and Tom opened the basket to reveal fresh bread, cheese, sliced ham, and two apples so red they looked painted. There was even a small jar of honey and—most luxurious of all—a bottle of elderflower cordial.

"Where did you get all this?" Annie asked, accepting the plate he handed her.

"Here and there. Mum helped with the bread. Jack's wife contributed the cheese. Billy's sister works at the orchard now." Tom looked slightly embarrassed. "I might have called in a few favors."

"For me?" The concept was still foreign, this web of care that had sprung up around her when she'd spent so long believing it was just her and her father against the world.

"For you," he confirmed simply.

Annie settled onto the blanket, still not quite believing the scene before her - the carefully arranged picnic, the gentle lapping of the river against its banks, and Tom Hartley sitting across from her with that expression that always made her stomach flutter traitorously.

"This is..." She paused, searching for words that wouldn't sound overly sentimental. "Unexpected."

Tom handed her a slice of bread topped with cheese and ham. "Good, unexpected, I hope?"

"Yes," she admitted, accepting the offering. "Very good, unexpected."

The first bite of food reminded Annie how hungry she'd been. Between the excitement of the court letter and preparing for this... whatever this was... she'd forgotten to eat since breakfast and lunch. The bread was still warm, the cheese sharp and creamy at once. It tasted like celebration.

"How's Mrs. Grant's order coming along?" Tom asked, pouring elderflower cordial into two mismatched cups.

"Nearly finished. Though she keeps adding requests. First it was new soles, then heel repairs, and yesterday she decided her granddaughter needs matching boots for her doll."

"Sounds profitable," Tom remarked, passing her a cup.

"Hardly. I'm charging her next to nothing, and the doll boots are a gift." Annie shook her head at her own softness. "But it's worth it to see her face light up when she talks about her granddaughter."

The cordial was sweet with just a hint of tartness, and Annie savored it as she watched the first stars prick the darkening sky. One by one they came out, like shy children from behind their mother's skirts. She couldn't remember the last time she'd simply sat and watched the stars appear.

"I've been thinking," she said suddenly. "Now that we're free of Drake, the shop has a real chance again."

Tom nodded encouragingly. "Your father's boots have always been the best in the county."

"Yes, but that's just it—boots and shoes aren't enough anymore." Annie set down her cup, warming to her subject. "Not with the factory prices being what they are. We need to diversify."

She hadn't realized how much thought she'd given this until she heard herself outlining it aloud.

The ideas had been forming in the back of her mind for weeks, perhaps months.

"I've been experimenting with smaller leather goods like coin purses, belts." Annie brushed a strand of hair behind her ear. "But I'm thinking we could offer ladies' handbags as well. The wealthy women who come for custom slippers are always carrying these fashionable bags from London. We could make similar styles with our own touches."

"That's brilliant, Annie."

"I'm also considering specialty riding boots for the gentry over in Thornfield. They pay a fortune to have them shipped from London, and half the time they don't fit properly. And then there's dancing slippers…"

"The kind the mayor's daughter wears?" Tom asked.

Annie nodded, pleased he'd remembered. "Exactly those. They're delicate work but high margin. And once father teaching me his patterns…"

"You'd be unstoppable," Tom finished with a grin.

"That is too much praise,"

The night air had cooled, but Annie felt warm through to her bones. How strange this was, to share aspirations she'd scarcely acknowledged to herself, and to have them met not with dismissal but with genuine support.

"It's a very good idea," Tom said, offering her a slice of apple. "With the fashion trends changing so quickly these days, having specialty items would set you apart from the general stores."

Annie accepted the apple, their fingers brushing momentarily. "That's what I thought. Though I'd never have considered it possible before... all this." She gestured vaguely.

"And what about you?" she asked, realizing how much of the conversation had centered on her plans. "Surely you're not planning to work those deadly shifts at the mill forever."

Tom leaned back on his elbows, his face half in shadow, half illuminated by the lantern light. "Actually, I've had some news of my own today."

Something in his tone made Annie's heart skip. "Good news, I hope?"

"The new management's restructuring the floor positions." Pride colored his voice. "They've asked me to take over as floor supervisor."

"Tom!" Annie's exclamation was genuine and warm. "That's wonderful."

"Better hours, better pay," he said with a modest

shrug that didn't quite hide his satisfaction. "And no more boiler room… ever."

Annie thought of his hands, raw and burned from those grueling night shifts, and felt a fierce gladness. "You deserve it. No one knows those looms better than you."

"They're bringing in some new safety measures too," Tom continued, clearly excited to share the details with someone who'd understand their significance. "Proper ventilation systems, and guards on the dangerous parts of the machines. Even talking about a medical office on-site."

"Your mother must be thrilled," Annie said, knowing how Sarah Hartley had worried herself sick over her son's dangerous work conditions.

Tom nodded. "She is. Though she's trying not to show it too much. Says she doesn't want me getting a swelled head."

Annie laughed, picturing Sarah's fond exasperation.

"She likes you, you know," Tom said suddenly. "She says you've got a good head on your shoulders and proper values."

Annie felt her cheeks heat but didn't look away. "I like her too."

They fell silent for a moment, the only sounds the gentle current of the river and the occasional night bird calling from the trees. Annie found she didn't mind the quiet between them. It felt comfortable, not awkward.

Tom broke the silence first. "The promotion means I can start saving properly. For a place of my own."

"Oh?" Annie tried to sound merely interested rather than intensely curious.

"Nothing grand," he hastened to add. "But something with a bit of garden space. For Mum, mainly. She's always wanted to grow her own herbs and vegetables instead of that pitiful window box at her cottage."

The image formed in Annie's mind, a small, tidy house with a garden plot, Sarah Hartley contentedly tending rows of thyme and sage, a far cry from the cramped cottage where she currently lived.

"That sounds lovely," she said softly.

"I thought..." He hesitated, fiddling with a blade of grass. "I thought maybe when it's ready, you might want to see it sometime."

Annie's breath caught slightly at the carefully casual way he said it. "I'd like that," she replied, equally casual though her pulse had quickened.

Tom nodded, a smile playing at the corners of his mouth. "Good."

As they finished the last of the cordial, Tom stretched out on his back, pointing up at the night sky.

"See there? That's Cassiopeia. Looks like a 'W' or an 'M' depending on how you tilt your head."

Annie lay beside him, following his gesture. "How do you know that?"

"My dad taught me. He said knowing the stars meant you could never truly be lost."

She turned her head to find him already looking at her, not at the stars at all. The intensity in his gaze made her breath catch.

"I was lost before I met you," he said quietly. "Working myself to death at the mill, taking care of Mum, just getting by. I wasn't living."

Annie swallowed hard. "I know what you mean. After Mum died, it was just survival for us. The shop, Father's health, the bills." She hesitated. "I didn't know how lonely I was until you started bringing in all those boots for repair."

Tom's laugh rumbled through the blanket between them. "I was running out of friends to borrow boots from."

"I suspected as much." She smiled, caught

between amusement and something deeper. "But I appreciated the effort."

He shifted onto his side to face her fully, his expression turning serious. "Annie Sutherland, I don't plan to stop making efforts where you're concerned."

The vulnerability in his voice undid her. All the walls she'd built since her mother's death, all the independence she'd clung to didn't stand a chance against the earnest honesty in Tom Hartley's eyes.

"Good," she whispered. "Because I'm counting on that."

His smile could have outshone the stars. Slowly, giving her every chance to pull away, he leaned forward and pressed his lips to hers. The kiss was soft, questioning, and over almost before it began. But it sent warmth through her like sunshine breaking through clouds after a long rain.

When they parted, neither of them spoke for a long moment.

"We should probably head back," Tom said eventually, though he made no move to rise. "I told your father we'd be home in time for supper."

Annie blinked. "You spoke to my father about this?"

"Of course." Tom looked puzzled. "I wouldn't take you off without his knowing."

She sat up, bewildered. "But you didn't mention supper before."

"Ah." Now he looked sheepish. "That was meant to be the second surprise. My mother's bringing over a roast chicken. Thought we might have a proper family dinner, the four of us."

Annie stared at him, this man who had apparently been orchestrating not just an evening for them, but a coming together of their families. Something her father hadn't experienced since her mother died—a proper meal with company, with laughter, with connection.

"Tom Hartley," she said, her voice slightly choked, "you are a marvel."

TOM

Tom stood at the threshold of the courthouse, his heart hammering against his ribs as he reread the letter for the fourth time. The county magistrate's seal gleamed at the bottom of the page. This letter was official, undeniable, and terrifying.

"Mr. Hartley, in recognition of your diligence and moral character in exposing corrupt business practices within our jurisdiction, we hereby offer you the position of Labor Practices Overseer for Mills County..."

The rest of the letter detailed responsibilities that made his palms sweat: inspecting factories, documenting working conditions, ensuring fair wages, investigating complaints. A position created specifically to prevent another Drake situation, with a salary that made his knees weak.

Five times what he made at the mill. Five times.

"They want your answer by Friday?" Jack Davidson asked, peering over Tom's shoulder.

Tom folded the letter carefully along its creases. "The new magistrate doesn't waste time."

"And neither should you." Jack clapped him on the shoulder, weathered face breaking into a rare smile. "Justice Matthews's made good on his promise to clean things up. Having one of our own watching over those fancy owners is what we need."

"I'm no lawman," Tom protested, though the seed of possibility had taken root the moment he'd broken the seal on the letter. "I've spent my life following orders, not giving them."

Jack snorted. "That's what you call organizing half the town to bring down Drake? Following orders?" He shook his head. "You've got something most men don't. You see what's wrong and can't look away. That's worth more than fancy schooling."

Tom tucked the letter into his jacket pocket, feeling its weight against his chest. "I need to think on it."

"Think quick," Jack called as Tom descended the

courthouse steps. "Opportunities like that don't knock twice."

But Tom wasn't heading home to think. His feet carried him toward High Street and a certain cobbler shop where the only opinion that truly mattered waited.

The bell above Sutherland's Cobbler Shop jingled as Tom stepped inside, the familiar scent of leather and beeswax washing over him like a welcome. Two customers stood at the counter.

Annie glanced up from where she knelt with a measuring tape, her practiced hands working around Mr. Hoskins' foot. The smile that bloomed across her face sent a rush of warmth through Tom's chest.

"I'll be with you shortly," she called, but there was a private note in her voice meant only for him, a small secret shared between them in a crowded room.

Tom nodded and moved to the workbench where Harold Sutherland sat stitching, his health improved enough these past weeks to work a few hours each day.

"Morning, sir," Tom said, removing his cap.

"Tom." Harold looked up, needle poised mid-stitch. "Didn't expect you until later. Thought you had business at the courthouse."

"I did. It's done now." Tom hesitated. "Actually, I was hoping to speak with Annie when she's free. Something important's come up."

Harold's eyes narrowed slightly, assessing. Then he nodded toward the back room. "Make yourself useful, then. Water's hot for tea."

He moved easily into the back room, familiar now with the small kitchen where he'd spent evenings these past weeks, sharing meals and conversation with the Sutherlands. He assembled the teapot and cups on the tray with the tin of biscuits Annie kept for special occasions.

When he returned, the shop had emptied. Annie stood behind the counter, tallying the day's earnings with ink-stained fingers. She looked up as he approached, a curious light in her green eyes.

"Tea in the middle of the day? Must be something serious." Her tone was light, but he caught the flicker of worry.

"Not bad serious," Tom assured her quickly. "Just... important."

"Dad's resting upstairs. Said his hands needed a break." She closed the ledger. "Which means he's giving us time alone. Subtle as a hammer, that man."

Tom smiled, setting the tray on the counter.

"Learned from the best, I suppose," he said, nodding toward her.

Annie laughed, the sound still rare and precious enough to make his heart skip. "Fair point." She poured tea into both cups. "So, what's this important matter?"

Tom reached into his pocket and withdrew the letter, placing it on the counter between them. "I've been offered a position."

Annie's brows rose as she picked up the letter, eyes widening as she scanned the contents. "Tom... this is..."

"Unexpected," he finished for her. "Terrifying, if I'm honest."

"It's perfect," she countered, looking up with bright eyes. "They want you to oversee working conditions and make sure the mill owners follow the law?"

He nodded, watching her carefully. "The pay's good. Better than good."

"And you're hesitating because...?" Her head tilted.

Tom ran a hand through his hair. "I'm a worker, Annie. Always have been taking orders, not giving them. What if I'm not qualified? What if I make things worse?"

Annie set the letter down with deliberate care. "Thomas Hartley," she said, using his full name in that way that always made him feel both scolded and cherished, "you organized an entire town to stand against a man who had the magistrate in his pocket. You've worked both the looms and the boiler room. You know every unsafe practice because you've survived them."

She reached across the counter to take his hand, her fingers warm and calloused against his. "Who better than someone who's felt the heat of those furnaces?"

Put that way, it did make a certain sense. "But what about my mother? I'll need to go to town more often. And you..." He stopped abruptly.

"Me?" Annie prompted. Tom swallowed hard. This wasn't how he'd planned it. Not here across a shop counter with tea growing cold between them. But Annie was looking at him with those clear green eyes, and suddenly the weight of the carved wooden ring in his other pocket seemed to burn through the fabric.

"I need to think about what's best for all of us," he said finally. "For our future."

A faint blush colored her cheeks. "I think," she

said carefully, "that we should talk about this somewhere that isn't my shop. Somewhere quiet."

Tom nodded, understanding. "The river? At dusk?"

Annie's lips curved. "I'll bring bread and cheese."

* * *

The river gleamed like spun gold as the sun's last rays caught the ripples and turned the ordinary water into something magical. Tom stood at the bank, skipping stones as he waited, each one sending concentric circles expanding across the surface.

He'd spent the afternoon with his mother, discussing the offer, planning how they might manage. She'd been tearfully supportive, pride shining in her eyes as she read the letter.

"Your father would have burst his buttons," she'd said, patting his cheek. "Though he'd never have admitted it."

As if every unexpected turn in his life, from his father's death to the mill to Drake's schemes, had been leading him precisely here, to this riverbank, to this sunset, to the sound of approaching footsteps behind him.

He turned to find Annie walking toward him, a

small basket over her arm, her hair loose around her shoulders instead of pinned up for work. She wore a simple blue dress he recognized as her mother's, altered to fit her slender frame. Something about seeing her this way, not as the hardworking cobbler but simply as Annie tightened his chest with a feeling too big for words.

"You're staring," she said as she reached him, but the smile playing at her lips told him she didn't mind.

"You're beautiful," he answered simply.

She ducked her head, still uncomfortable with compliments. "I brought more than bread and cheese," she said, nodding toward the basket. "Mrs. Peters had jam tarts left over. Said they'd only go stale otherwise."

"Molly's mother bringing us dessert?" Tom raised an eyebrow. "Should I be worried she knows we're meeting alone?"

Annie laughed, setting the basket down on a flat rock near the water. "The whole town knows we're meeting, Tom. Nothing stays secret long." She settled beside the basket, arranging her skirts. "Dad asked if we'd be home before midnight."

"And what did you tell him?" Tom joined her on the rock, close enough that their shoulders brushed.

"That it depends on what you have to say." She looked at him sideways, a challenge in her gaze.

Tom took a deep breath. "I'm taking the position."

Annie's face broke into a brilliant smile. "I knew you would."

"Did you now?" He nudged her gently with his elbow. "That certain of me?"

"I know you," she said simply. "You couldn't walk away from a chance to make things better, even if it terrifies you."

"It won't be easy," he admitted. "I'll make enemies. The mill owners won't like someone poking around their operations, asking questions."

"Good," Annie said fiercely. "They should be nervous. Things need to change."

Tom reached for her hand, twining his fingers with hers. "And what about us? Will we change too?"

Annie stilled, her eyes searching his face. "What do you mean?"

Tom reached into his pocket with his free hand and withdrew a small wooden ring. He'd carved it himself over several nights, sanding it smooth, polishing it until the grain glowed. It wasn't gold or silver, those would come later, when he could afford them.

"I mean this," he said, holding it between them. "I

mean that I love you, Annie Sutherland. That I want to build a life with you."

Annie's eyes widened as they fixed on the ring.

"It's not much," he continued quickly. "Not yet. But I promise you this: I will work every day to make a home worthy of you. To be a husband worthy of you."

"Tom..." Her voice was barely above a whisper.

"I know it's fast," he said, suddenly uncertain. "If you need time..."

Annie shook her head, cutting him off. "It's not fast. And yes, Tom Hartley. Yes, I will marry you."

Relief and joy crashed through him like a wave. Tom slipped the ring onto her finger, where it fit perfectly, he'd spent hours estimating the size, terrified of getting it wrong.

"It's beautiful," Annie whispered, turning her hand to admire the simple band. "You made this?"

"I wanted it to be something real. Something that came from my hands to yours." Tom brushed a strand of hair from her face, letting his fingers linger against her cheek. "Like everything between us."

Annie leaned into his touch, her eyes fluttering closed. "I wouldn't have it any other way."

Tom drew her closer and kissed her. Annie

wound her arms around his neck, and Tom held her as if she might dissolve into the dusk if he let go.

When they finally broke apart, breathless, the first stars had appeared above them. Annie rested her forehead against his, her smile so close he could feel it more than see it.

"So," she murmured, "what do we tell my father when we get back?"

Tom laughed softly. "The truth. That his daughter has agreed to marry a former mill worker turned county official."

"And that we're happy," Annie added, her voice steady and sure. "Truly happy."

EPILOGUE

Annie stood at the workbench, needle flashing in the morning light that streamed through the freshly cleaned windows of Sutherland's Cobbler Shop. A year had turned the space from a dusty, desperate place to something bursting. The shelves that once stood barren now held rows of boots in various stages of completion, each pair tagged with a customer's name.

She flexed her fingers, working out a small cramp. Three pairs finished before lunch was not bad. The bell above the door jingled, and Annie looked up to see Mrs. Fletcher come in, her arms laden with packages.

"Good morning, Mrs. Fletcher," Annie said, wiping her hands on her apron.

"Annie, dear! I've brought those buttons you asked about... oh, and some of my apple tarts. Can't have you working all morning without something sweet."

Annie accepted the offerings, her stomach giving a traitorous little rumble at the sight of the tarts. "You're too kind. You know you don't need to keep feeding me."

"Nonsense. A working woman needs sustenance." Mrs. Fletcher's eyes twinkled. "Especially one keeping half the town well-shod. My Herbert says those boots you made him last winter are the finest he's ever owned."

Pride flickered through Annie's chest, a feeling that had become familiar but no less sweet over the past year. "Tis father's design, and my stitching. We make a good team."

"Speaking of Harold, how is he today?"

Annie gestured toward the small sitting area they'd added at the front of the shop, where her father sat with Mr. Nelson, the pair hunched over some sketches. "See for yourself. Semi-retired but can't quite let go."

Harold Sutherland's health had improved remarkably once the weight of imminent ruin had lifted. Though he still coughed in the mornings and tired easily, he'd found a new role as the shop's designer and mentor to the two apprentices they'd taken on. His latest sketches for ladies' walking boots had orders backed up for three weeks.

"Those two plotting another revolution in footwear?" Mrs. Fletcher laughed.

"Something about articulated ankle support. I've learned not to question the genius," Annie said with a wink. "Now, let me see those buttons. I think they'll be perfect for Mrs. Mayor's dress boots."

As Mrs. Fletcher departed, and Annie returned to her work. Her hands drifted briefly to her abdomen, still flat beneath her apron. Seven weeks along, Dr. Perkins had confirmed yesterday. Their little secret for now, though not for much longer. She and Tom had agreed to share the news at today's dinner.

The thought of Tom brought another smile to her face. Her husband, still a word that made her heart skip, would be finishing his inspections at Harding's Mill about now. In his year as Labor Practices Overseer, he'd transformed conditions across three counties, with shorter hours for children, safety improvements, and fair wage agreements. The bell jingled again, and Annie glanced up, hoping it might be Tom stopping by early. Instead, Molly burst in, cheeks flushed.

"You'll never guess what Ben's mother is bringing today," she said without preamble, dropping onto the stool beside Annie's workbench.

"Hello to you too," Annie replied dryly, but couldn't suppress her smile. Marriage had mellowed many things about her, but her dry wit wasn't one of them.

"Sorry, hello, good morning, how are you, the sun is shining," Molly rattled off. "Now can I tell you about the monstrosity of a pudding she's inflicting on us all?"

Annie bit back a laugh. "By all means."

As Molly launched into a detailed description of her mother-in-law's culinary sins, Annie stitched and nodded, grateful for the friendship that had only deepened since they'd both married. Molly and Ben Adams had wed just two months after Annie and Tom, a quiet ceremony at St. Mark's following a whirlwind courtship.

"... and then she said, 'Well, I suppose some young wives simply haven't mastered proper homemaking yet,' and I nearly stuck her with my needle right there in the sewing circle!"

"Please don't commit violence at my dinner table," Annie said mildly. "I just got those new linens."

Molly sighed dramatically. "Fine. For your linens,

I'll behave." She leaned closer, lowering her voice. "Are you telling everyone today?"

Annie nodded, her eyes flicking to ensure her father was still engrossed in conversation. "After dinner. Tom's so excited he's practically vibrating."

"Ben's going to demand you name it after him, you know."

"Absolutely not. Can you imagine Tom's face if we named our child Benedict Adams Hartley?"

Both women dissolved into laughter, drawing curious glances from James their apprentice.

"Back to work, you," Annie told him, straightening her face into what Tom called her 'formidable proprietress' expression.

* * *

HOME. The word still gave her a little thrill. Their cottage sat just off High Street, a ten-minute walk from the shop. It was nothing grand. It was two bedrooms, a cozy sitting room, and a kitchen with the luxury of a pump right indoors, but it was theirs.

The front garden bloomed with summer flowers, Tom's mother's influence evident in the neat rows and creative arrangements. Annie paused to deadhead a few spent blooms before pushing open the door.

"Tom?" she called.

"Out back!" came the reply.

She followed the sound through the house and out the back door, where the workshop stood. He'd built it himself over the winter, a sturdy structure where logs and planks became furniture under his increasingly skilled hands. The carpentry had started as a way to furnish their home without expense, but it had quickly grown into a side business as neighbors admired his craftsmanship.

She found him bent over his workbench, sanding the curved leg of what appeared to be a cradle.

"Starting early, aren't we?" she said, leaning against the doorframe.

Tom looked up, a smile breaking across his face. No matter how many times she saw it, that smile still did something peculiar to her insides.

"Just being prepared," he replied, setting down his tools and crossing to her. His hands, rough with calluses, came to rest gently on her waist. "How are you feeling?"

"Perfectly fine. No sickness today. Your mother's tea might actually be working."

He kissed her forehead, then her lips. "Good. I was worried about you standing all day at the shop."

Annie pulled back, giving him a look. "Thomas Hartley, we've discussed this. I'm pregnant, not made of glass. Women have been making boots while carrying babies since the beginning of time."

"I know, I know." He held up his hands in surrender. "Forgive a man for fussing over his wife."

She softened, leaning into him. "You're forgiven. This time." She nodded toward the cradle. "It's beautiful."

Pride flickered across his face. "It's not finished yet. I'm thinking cherry wood for the rockers will gives it a nice contrast."

"It'll be perfect." She glanced back toward the house. "We should start preparing. Everyone will be here in a few hours."

Tom nodded, brushing sawdust from his shirt. "I'll clean up here and come help. Just let me finish this section while the idea's fresh."

Annie watched Tom return to his work, his broad shoulders flexing as he bent over the cradle. There was something mesmerizing about watching him work.

She lingered in the doorway longer than she'd intended, remembering how those same hands had held hers at the altar of St. Mark's, how they'd trembled slightly as he slid the simple gold band onto her finger. How different her life had become since that day.

"You're staring," Tom said without looking up, a smile in his voice.

"I'm appreciating," Annie corrected, feeling a blush creep up her neck. "There's a difference."

He turned then with sawdust clinging to his forearms. "Appreciating what, exactly?"

"The craftsmanship," she replied primly, though the effect was ruined by her own rebellious smile. "It's an excellent joinery."

Tom set down his tools and crossed the workshop in three strides. "Is that right? The joinery?"

"Mmm. Very precise work." Annie tilted her head back to look up at him, no longer bothering to hide her smile. "Though I suppose the craftsman himself isn't entirely without merit."

His laugh came warm against her cheek as he wrapped his arms around her waist, drawing her closer. "High praise from Sutherland's finest cobbler."

"Hartley," she corrected softly. "Annie Hartley now."

The name still felt new on her tongue, still gave

her a small thrill to say aloud. For all her initial resistance to changing anything about herself or her life, she'd found she didn't mind this particular change at all.

"Annie Hartley," Tom repeated, his voice dropping to a low tone that never failed to send a pleasant shiver down her spine. "My wife."

ALSO BY SYBIL COOK

The Farrier's Daughter

In a world defined by duty and hardship, can love be the escape that leads to a future worth fighting for?

In the heart of the English countryside, Enid Boothe's life is shaped by duty and hardship. As the daughter of a farrier, she helps care for her many siblings while managing the demands of a humble home. With sickness and financial struggle weighing heavily on the family, Enid's world begins to shift when she meets Jack Greenwood, a young groundsman at the nearby Braley House. Despite her deep sense of responsibility and the turmoil at home, Enid is drawn to Jack's kindness and the lightness he brings to her otherwise grim life.

As their bond grows, so does the pressure on Enid's family. When her father loses his job and her mother's health declines, Enid is forced to confront the impossible choice between caring for her family and pursuing the future she dreams of with Jack. Just as things seem hopeless, a chance opportunity at the Big House offers Enid a new path forward, but it comes at the cost of her dreams of escape.

As Enid learns new skills and supports her family, her

love for Jack continues to grow. With her father finding new work and the weight of their struggles finally easing, Enid and Jack's love story blooms into a future neither of them ever thought possible. But will Enid's loyalty to her family and her desire for a better life collide, or will love and perseverance lead them to a brighter future?

DOWNLOAD NOW

Printed in Great Britain
by Amazon